From a young age, Nyrae Dawn dreamed of growing up and writing stories. For years she put her dream on hold. Nyrae worked in a hospital emergency room, fell in love and married one of her best friends from high school. In 2004 Nyrae, her husband and their new baby girl made a move from Oregon to Southern California and that's when everything changed. As a stay-at-home mom for the first time, her passion for writing flared to life again. She hasn't stopped writing since. With two incredible daughters, an awesome husband and her days spent writing what she loves, Nyrae considers herself the luckiest girl in the world. She still resides in sunny Southern California, where she loves spending time with her family and sneaking away to the bookstore with her laptop. Nyrae Dawn also writes adult romance under the name Kelley Vitollo.

To find out more about Nyrae Dawn, visit www.nyraedawn.com. Find her on Facebook at nyraedawnwrites and follow her on Twitter @NyraeDawn.

ALSO BY NYRAE DAWN AND
PUBLISHED BY HEADLINE ETERNAL

What a Boy Wants
What a Boy Needs

THE GAMES TRILOGY
Charade
Façade

Nyrae Dawn

WHAT A BOY NEEDS

headline
ETERNAL

First published in Great Britain in 2013 by HEADLINE ETERNAL
An imprint of HEADLINE PUBLISHING GROUP

1

Cataloguing in Publication Data is available from the British Library

ISBN 978 1 4722 0876 7

Typeset in Electra by Palimpsest Book Production Limited,
Falkirk, Stirlingshire

Printed and bound by CPI Group
(UK) Ltd, Croydon, CR0 4YY

Headline's policy is to use papers that are natural, renewable
and recyclable products and made from wood grown in sustainable
forests. The logging and manufacturing processes are expected to
conform to the environmental regulations of the country of origin.

HEADLINE PUBLISHING GROUP
An Hachette UK Company
338 Euston Road
London NW1 3BH

www.eternalromancebooks.co.uk
www.headline.co.uk
www.hachette.co.uk

Jaden's story is dedicated to the people who took a chance on Sebastian and his story. I have been blessed with the most incredible readers in the world. Your passion and support for these four characters means more to me than I can say. Sebastian, Aspen, Jaden, Pris and I wouldn't be where we are without you.

Also, to the boys I was friends with in high school. You guys were crazy, wild, funny and got into trouble – but you were also loyal, protective and some of the best friends I've ever had. I thought about you often while writing Sebastian and Jaden's stories.

And, lastly, to my husband. You were one of the boys I'm talking about above. How did we get so lucky?

ACKNOWLEDGEMENTS

HUGE thank-you to my family for not ditching me when I'm deep in a story. My kids for understanding. My husband for listening to me talk about these characters often and for at least pretending to 'get it'.

My mom, who thinks I can do anything and actually makes me believe it.

My Trio of Awesomeness: Wendy Higgins, you are all heart, like me. I know I can always go to you with matters of the heart and you will understand. So awesome. Jolene Perry who gets just as excited about things as I do. When I need someone to take a 'jump' with me, it's you. We might gripe at ourselves later for not thinking it through, but at least we did it together! And Kelley York who is my voice of reason. You are always logical and reel me in when I look at things with my heart that I should examine with my head instead. I could not write a book without you, ladies. You're the best critique partners a girl could ask for.

Also to Jessica Skondin, Steph Campbell, Jen and Kristy Zavorka for reading.

Last, but definitely not least, to Valerie, Andrea, Autumn and Amber. Thanks for everything. I feel so blessed to have met and made friends with you!

CHAPTER ONE

I stiffen. Heat rips through my body like someone injected it into my veins. It starts in my chest, cracking and crystalizing my insides as it spreads. There's a part of me, the smart part, that knows I'm being an idiot. I'm freaking out when I don't have a right to. But there's the other part, the one that hides deep inside of me so I can pretend it doesn't exist, that knows it should be *me* sitting with Priscilla right now. My hand in her hair. My lips on her neck. I should be stealing food off her lunch plate and saying something stupid because it's so like *us* for her to be pissed at me.

I've been making her mad ever since that time in kindergarten when she yelled at me for Sebastian's lame ass pulling Aspen's ponytail. Aspen started chasing Bastian like she was supposed to, since he's the one who did it, but Pris narrowed those dark eyes at me like it was my fault, before she charged.

I let her catch me.

I like it when she catches me.

But last summer, she stopped chasing. It sucks.

So does my internal monologue every time I see her. It's really starting to piss me off. I've gone soft and I hate it, but I can't seem to make myself do anything about it, either. Instead I grin, talk shit to Bastian, tease Aspen, and pretend it doesn't tear me up every time I look at her. That I don't know it's my own damn fault, and that there's nothing I can do to change it. It's for the best.

In case you haven't caught on, it's been a long school year.

The Pris-dating-Craig thing is new, but it doesn't feel like it.

I want my fist to meet his nose. Multiple times.

Aren't I just peachy?

I've become a serious buzz kill. Priscilla, Sebastian, Aspen, and I have been tight forever. It's always been the four of us, but last summer Sebastian fell for Aspen. It was only a matter of time anyway and it's cool. I'm happy for them and all that, but it's made stuff for Priscilla and me tough because I want to be with her, too. I want her way more than I should, but I also realize it's a no go. She deserves way better. For her sake, I hate that it took her so long to realize it.

Someone slams into my back, making me stumble. I whip around and take a swing at Sebastian, which he dodges, bouncing on the balls of his feet to try and look like he's some kind of heavyweight boxer.

"Don't make me take you out, *Doc*," I tease. The whole thing with him and Aspen started because Sebastian ran some stupid, anonymous business online where he called himself the Hook-up Doctor. Aspen contacted him to hook her up with this idiot who used to work at the pizza place with them, only he didn't know it was her and she didn't know it was him. He started to fall for her and everything was all set for a movie-ending happily ever after until he pulled a bonehead-Sebastian move.

It all worked out in the end because if he wasn't so blind, he would have known they wanted each other probably since that day in kindergarten. Priscilla and I were his only failed hook-up.

I slam the door on those thoughts.

"Please, I could take you with my eyes closed—shit, ouch." Sebastian limps after accidentally stepping on Aspen's foot.

"Hello? *You* stepped on *me*. I should be the one saying ouch!" She pushes a strand of her light brown hair behind her ear. Sebastian buries his face in her neck the same way Craig just did with Pris. Aspen's hand threads through his black hair.

"Sorry, baby." Bastian leans forward. "Gimme a kiss. My lips have healing power."

Aspen swoons and I almost vomit in my mouth. "Healing power? Did I mention I fell on my ass this

3

morning? It hurts right here." I turn and point to my left cheek. Sebastian tries to kick me, but I jerk out of his way, laughing.

"Ha, ha." He smirks. He knows that was a good joke. He just doesn't want to admit it.

"You're just jealous I thought of it."

We fall in line together as the three of us head toward Priscilla at our table. Pris sitting with her boyfriend at the table that's belonged to the four of us since our freshman year.

Seriously, it's like I can't stop those little comments from body-slamming their way into my brain. This isn't supposed to be the way it works. I'm not sure *how* it was supposed to work since I've always known I couldn't go there. Not with her, even though she makes my pulse jack-hammer. But before, I could ignore it. After all the shit went down with Aspen and Sebastian last summer—after I found out she tried to find a way to make me see her in a different light—it makes things a whole hell of a lot harder to ignore.

I've always seen her. Always.

I've just been trying not to.

"What's up?" I fall onto the bench across from them. I give her a little nod, but don't pay attention to the douche. Really? Craig? He's always been a clown. I don't know what she sees in him.

4

After twisting the top off my Cherry Pepsi, I down a drink.

"Hey, Jay," Pris replies, but gives her attention to Aspen. "Did you finish your math homework?"

"Pris, you realize we graduate in two weeks, right?" Sebastian cuts in. "I'm pretty sure there's a coolness rule that says you're not supposed to do homework anymore. It's expected and shit."

Aspen nudges him. "*I* did my homework."

"Guess Jay and I are the only cool ones, then."

We hit fists. "Not really a newsflash, B." We both laugh while the girls roll their eyes like they always do. Craig's on his phone playing whatever his game of the week is. He's always on his phone when he's around us. It might or might not be because Sebastian and I don't really pay any attention to him. Probably not a very cool thing to do, but I seriously can't stand to look at the guy and Bastian's just tight like that. He's my boy and it's in our code to always have each other's backs. I'm sure he's cool to Craig when I'm not around, but just like I never would have been tight with Mattie, the guy Aspen got with for a little bit last year, Bastian wouldn't hang me out to dry either.

Plus, I'm pretty sure Craig dislikes us as much as we dislike him.

Something catches my eye and I look over to see

5

Craig pull out a pack of gum and push a piece of spearmint into his mouth.

"Want one, Priscilla?" He holds the pack out to her.

Hearing him call her Priscilla makes me want to go nuts.

Douche.

The way Sebastian smirks and turns his head to look at me, I realize I must have said that out loud. Oops. Not.

"Jaden!" Priscilla's voice is tight. It's different when she's mad at me now. Before it was just *us* and it was never real anger and now it's . . . hell, I don't know. It's just different.

She turns to Craig and takes the piece of gum he offered her. I can't believe she actually puts it in her mouth, just to spite me.

Yep. That's my cue to get out of here.

I push to my feet. "See ya after school, Bastian." I turn to Craig. "Ever since she got sick off Peppermint Schnapps last year, Spearmint makes her feel like she's going to puke."

I shove my hands into my pockets. Without another word, I'm out.

"What was up at lunch today?" Sebastian asks as I lean the seat back in his SUV. After everything went down last summer, his mom made him keep the job at the pizza place. He'd been saving for a car, but a couple months ago his mom and her new husband Roger bought this for him. They want him to save his money for New York this summer. He's going to school to study music and the girls are going to NYU. For years we've planned for all of us to go out there after high school.

My gut clenches thinking about it, but I push it aside and focus on the fact that it's cool Bastian gets to cart my ass around now instead of the other way around.

What did he ask me? Oh, yeah. Lunch. "Umm, I ate it? That's typically what happens at lunch. In fact, I hear it's the whole concept." I smirk as I play with the ring in my bottom lip. I have one in my eyebrow too, a fact that my asshole of a . . . dad hates. I hate even using the name "Dad" for him because it's not what he acts like.

It's part of the reason I like the piercings.

"You know what I'm talking about, Captain Avoid-an-Answer. The whole calling Pris's boyfriend a douche and then bailing."

I look at him. "He *is* a douche."

"He is, but you gotta pick the time and place to call him on it. All you're doing is pissing off Pris."

I want to bang my head into the glass. It shouldn't

7

be this way. Sebastian isn't supposed to be the level-headed one who actually sounds like he knows what he's talking about. But I know he's right. It's like I can't stop myself though.

Why the hell did everything have to go down like it did last summer?

Bastian realizing he loved Aspen.

Finding out Priscilla wanted to try and hook up with me.

And that it didn't change a thing.

"I know."

Sebastian takes a right, heading toward my driveway. "Dude . . . You like her. You won't admit it, but I know you do. Seriously, why don't you just—"

"Not going there." I feel his eyes on me and it makes me feel like a pussy. "Sorry, not all of us want a ball and chain at eighteen. There are way too many girls out there to—"

"When's the last time you hooked up?"

"Huh?" His question surprises me. He's not usually one to talk about hook-ups.

"You heard me, Goldilocks. When's the last time you kissed a girl? Hooked up at a party? Went out?"

I drop my head against the headrest and close my eyes. Damn him for falling in love with Aspen and suddenly wanting to talk about important stuff. The fact is, I'm not really feelin' it anymore. I mean, it was cool when it was the two of us—when I didn't know who it hurt, but it doesn't feel the same anymore.

I'm not gonna lie; I did meet a girl at a party right after Priscilla got with Craig, but it didn't feel like it used to. Ever since that party on her birthday last summer, nothing has felt the same. I pretend it does. Do a pretty good job of it, most of the time.

"Maybe I just don't tell you about it since you're all happily married and stuff."

Sebastian laughs. "I'm being real, Jay. What's up?"

Luckily we pull into my driveway right as he asks me that. "Nothing's up. Maybe I'll have to rectify my lack of hook-ups tonight." I get out of the car, slamming the door behind me.

Each step I take toward my house makes my gut churn more. I hate this place and can't wait to be out of here. Again, that makes me think of New York—how we're supposed to take this huge road trip out there in a couple weeks. It used to be all we talked about, but I think everyone knows it's going to be different now. I've always been a little more on the outside with my friends. I mean, not really, but Sebastian has this kickass mom. Aspen's parents are a little nutty, but they're cool. Priscilla's parents aren't around as much as the others, but they give her everything she wants. Stuff she probably doesn't want, too.

Me? Let's just say when the group went camping, it was always with Aspen's parents. When we got something cool, it was because Priscilla's parents got it for her. When we need a place to stay or even something as small as a cooked meal, we went to Sebastian's mom.

My parents have never been in the equation.

Now Bastian and Aspen are together. Priscilla has the douche.

And then there's me.

I push the front door open and close it quietly behind me. Mom's in the kitchen washing dishes. I'm not sure where my dad is.

"Hi. How was your day?" she asks.

"All right." I don't bother telling her I'm going out tonight, because I know it doesn't matter. I'm sure things are easier on her when I'm not around anyway.

"You left your clothes in the dryer this morning. Make sure you don't forget them anymore, okay? Your dad had to take them out for you."

Oh no. Wouldn't want him to have to lift a finger when it comes to me. "I'm sure that was a real hardship for him. You know, moving clothes for his son, and all."

"Jaden." She doesn't get a chance to finish speaking because the front door slams.

Great. He's home. I hoped I wouldn't have to see him today.

He struts over to her and grabs her by the hips. I think he steps hard on purpose, like it makes him sound strong or something.

"How's my woman today?" he asks before kissing her.

"Wonderful. Did you have a good day at work?" She's actually smiling at him.

He doesn't spare me a glance as he talks to her. Doesn't say excuse me as he pushes around me, his shoulder hitting mine.

On purpose.

And she doesn't call him on it. Not that it would matter if she did. And not like I wouldn't rather him pretend I'm not here anyway.

Neither of them notice or care as I walk out of the room.

CHAPTER TWO

I stand in front of my mirror. It's stupid but it still feels weird to see my hair light brown. I stopped bleaching it this year. Without thinking about it, I take out the ring in my eyebrow. I don't know why I do it, but I put on the one Priscilla got me for my birthday last fall. It's a silver bar with studs on each end. It's nothing special, but it's one I mentioned liking months before. She could have afforded to get me anything, but she got me a ten-dollar stud that she remembered I liked because she knew it was *me* more than anything else.

Which shouldn't be a big deal, but it is. I swear I've suddenly turned into a sentimental sap that I would have made fun of two years ago.

"Aww, aren't you pretty wearing all that jewelry. Are you sure you don't want to wear a dress, too?" Dad's voice is low, steady.

My whole body stiffens as I try to ignore him.

"Too good to answer me like you're too good to fold your own clothes?"

I can't even say his voice is slurred because he's

been drinking or anything like that. The fact is, he just hates me. He always has. Too bad I don't know why. "It's really not that big a deal. It was an accident. It won't happen again."

He laughs. I look behind me to see his beefy arms crossed over his chest as he leans in my doorway. My fists tighten. What would it be like to punch him? To physically repay him for all the words he's jammed into my skull for all these years?

"That's right! You think you're going to New York with your friends soon, right? How are you going to do that? Mooch off them? I know you don't have any money and you sure as hell aren't getting anymore of mine. Eighteen years is enough of that. Pretty soon they'll get tired of picking up your slack, kid. It won't take them long to realize what I've always known. You're not worth it. You're not worth anything."

His words hit home everything I already know. They fill me up, echo in my head until I want nothing more than to break something. Anything. Everything.

"They won't have to pay my way. I can get a job, and for school they're called scholarships. Maybe you've heard of them?" I never used to talk back to him. Never. Last year when things started to get worse though, I realized it didn't matter. Nothing I did would change him. I would never be good enough regardless, so why take it silently?

"Watch your mouth, boy."

This time, I ignore him. It makes him madder than when I talk back.

But the shitty part is, he's right. I'm not going into this situation the same way my friends are. The beater's engine died which means I don't even have that one thing Bastian used to need. My parents didn't put money away for me like Aspen and Sebastian's. Mine don't have more money than God like Priscilla's and if they did, they wouldn't share it with me. How long will the couple grand I saved last?

I fight to shake those thoughts from my head. It's not like he's telling me anything I haven't known forever. Funny how you can fool yourself. I used to think everything would work out. We would all make the trip and things would change for me. I would be more than the Jaden I am now. The older I get, the more I know that's not gonna happen. How long will it take me to get a job? The scholarships I applied for, I didn't get. I'm not like the rest of them . . . I'm not even sure what I want to do yet.

He steps into the room. He's never put his hands on me. Sometimes I think it would be easier to deal with than his words that still rot inside me long after physical wounds would heal.

"You think you have all the answers, don't you, smartass? One of these days you're going to wake up and realize you're nothing. You think you're a man, but real men don't put holes in their faces and dress like bums. You're nothing but the product of—"

"Mike, do you want to come watch a movie with me? I made some popcorn for you," Mom's voice cuts him off. Not "don't talk to my son that way." Not "get the fuck out of my house." It's "I made you popcorn. Come hang out with me."

I turn away from them. My nails bite into my hand because my fist is so tight. I can't fucking wait to get out of here.

Once in a while our foursome becomes a threesome. We always used to go to parties together, but now Pris goes with Craig and I get stuck with the love doctor and Aspen. Totally not my idea of a good time. Especially when you can tell they're trying to be extra friendly to me like they're afraid I'm going to break down and cry.

And they wonder why I haven't talked to them about what goes on in my life. Not that I don't think they get it on some level, but I'm already sick of the poor-Jaden looks. Add to it that I'm pretty sure they both know the Pris thing makes me want to go all Incredible Hulk and tear stuff up, and yeah . . . so not doing the talking thing.

"I hear there's going to be a ton of people here tonight," Aspen says. "Should be a good time."

"Definitely looking forward to having some fun and meeting a girl or two."

I don't need a light in the car to know she's giving me a sad look. Whatever. For once I'm being totally honest. I'm done with the monk routine I've been playing the past few months. I'm done with it all. It hasn't done me any good anyway. I turn my hat around backward. Girls are always talking about my eyes. Might as well show them off.

We get to the house about five minutes later. Sebastian does his park-a-block-away thing, because it's always easier to bail that way if the cops break up the party, and we start for the house.

"Do you realize this is probably one of the last parties we'll have here? We're about to graduate. After that, we're going to New York. We def need to go out with a bang." Bastian nudges me.

"You're such a douche," I tease. He's always been into everything being epic, huge. It's gotten us into trouble more times than I can count and while I'm totally down with what he's saying, I also have to give him crap about it too.

Well, I agree with the going-out-with-a-bang part. The New York gig I both dread and can't wait for.

A slap-boxing match suddenly breaks out between

us before Aspen jumps in the middle to make us stop. Sebastian pulls her to him and gives her a kiss, and I just stand there like the douche I just called him. This used to be where, instead of kissing, they'd get into a silly argument. And then Pris would start in on me. Now I'm sitting here like an idiot who is totally getting annoyed with his own thoughts. Why does everything always go back to her?

"You gonna let me in on that?" I pretend to try to pull Aspen away from him. "I'm a much better kisser than he is."

She swats me. "And how do you know that, huh? Is there something I need to know about?"

"Sebastian couldn't handle me." I put her in a loose headlock and mess up her hair.

"Jaden!" She easily slips away from me. "You just messed up my hair!"

"That was the plan." Both Sebastian and I start to laugh and then we're heading for the house again.

"Pris just texted. She wants us to meet her by the back door for the PPP." Aspen slips her phone into her pocket.

We started the pre-party plan a few years ago. We always had a plan for who would drive, what time to have meet-ups, etc. We may give each other crap a lot, but we always had each other's backs. Even when she went to a party with Craig, we made sure to have the PPP. Only tonight . . . tonight, I don't know why, but I can't deal with it. Can't deal with seeing her.

My dad's words beat down on me, *"You're not worth anything . . ."* If I'm not even good enough for that prick, there's no way I'd ever be good enough for a girl like her. I've always known that, but somehow the words feel more real tonight.

"I'm cool. I'll text you guys if I need you." I start to walk away, but Sebastian grabs my arm.

"Umm . . . you're screwing with our mojo here. We always do this."

I shrug and pull my arm away. "We don't really need to anymore. Aspen has you to take care of her and Pris has Craig. Bases covered." I don't look back to see his reaction.

Pushing through the door, I start to shoulder my way through the crowd. It's packed. So crazy busy it's hard to even walk through the place. Just what I needed. I head straight for the kitchen, find the keg and hand over my cup fee to the keg monitor. I give him enough for two cups, which he marks so everyone knows I purchased, fills them, and hands them over.

I drink both cups before getting two more. I'm good and buzzed not long after getting here. For a second I let myself wonder if they met up with Pris and got the PPP out of the way. No matter what I said, I definitely don't want to leave her in the hands of *Craig*.

And, on that note, it's time to move on. I'm heading toward the living room, where the music is playing. People are dancing on couches, tables, the floor. I stumble a little when someone runs into me. I turn to tell whoever it is to watch out, but big, green eyes look up at me and a pair of thin lips stretch into a smile.

Jackpot.

"How'd I get so lucky to have you run into me?" Yeah, I know. I'm laying it on thick and it's actually ridiculous, but her smile grows wider.

"Hi." Her cheeks turn a light shade of pink.

"I'm Jaden. What's your name?"

"Samantha."

"You here with anyone?"

"Just my friends."

"Wanna dance?"

"Definitely." She starts to lose some of her shyness when I pull her into my arms and start to dance with her. Is it a slow song? Nope, but what's the point in dancing if you're not close when you do it?

Samantha and I move together to the music. Her arms wrap around my neck and sit under the bill of my hat. Her waist is small, thin, and for a second Pris pops into my head. They're so different, these two. She's got that smooth, dark skin where this girl is lighter. She's curvier. I remember her and Aspen arguing about it once. Pris was doing that girl thing of thinking she was fat.

I wanted to tell her, screw that. Curves are hot. But yeah . . . of course, I didn't.

"Do you go to school here?" I ask Samantha against her ear. "I don't remember seeing you."

"No . . . I'm one town over."

We keep dancing until the song ends and keep moving into the next one. Once it's over, I reach for her hand and lead her to the quietest corner we can find. It feels wrong, but I'm trying to move on, so I lean forward, cupping her cheek with my hand. But then . . . she gives me that sweet smile. The one that says she's looking for a boyfriend and I'm *totally* not looking for a girlfriend.

Sebastian and I have met tons of girls over the past few years, but neither of us has ever been down with the playing-them-thing. It's not how I roll. "I really want to kiss you right now, but I gotta tell you, I'm just trying to have fun. I'm not looking for anything more.

The lips I just wanted to kiss turn downward and I know I'm losing her. "I'm not into random hook-ups."

I pull my hand away, strangely okay with it.

"Thanks for being honest, though. Most guys wouldn't."

I give her my best smile and a wink. "I'm not most guys."

She laughs, giving me an "A" for my fake effort.

I pull off my hat and scratch my head, trying to figure out what to say. I shove it back on my head and keep going with the honesty thing. "I'm gonna go, okay? I'll see you around, sometime." I'm not trying to be a jerk, but go figure. I am.

Samantha looks down at the ground. "See ya around."

"Thanks for the dance."

And just like that, she's walking away. As I watch her, my eyes catch familiar black hair. It's long, straight, and moving way too fast as Pris shoves her way toward the door.

My heart starts to jackhammer as I push my way toward her. She's heading for the kitchen, then the backdoor.

"Pris!" There's no way she can hear me over the music and the people. I still can't stop myself from trying. "Pris, wait up!"

She's out the door when I see Aspen and Sebastian run out behind her. I don't even know where they came from. I can hardly breathe as I run through the doorway and into the backyard. I see Pris and Aspen off toward the back of the yard, in a corner by some trees and I head straight for them.

"What happened?"

Pris's eyes find mine and they're red. I start to *see*

red, too. "What did he do? Did that douchebag hurt you?"

My words seem to upset her more. "I can't . . . I can't do this with you, Jaden. Not with him here." And then she turns, burying her face in Aspen's shoulder.

My stomach drops.

My hands tighten into fists even more fierce than the ones at my house early.

Sebastian throws a hand over my shoulder. "Come on, bro. I think they need girl time, or whatever."

My body is too tight. My muscles are frozen, making myself unable to move. "What happened?"

"I don't know . . . From what I heard it sounds like they were in the room. He started to get a little too touchy-feely and she told him to slow down and he just dumped her or something."

"Bastian! Come here. I need your help." Aspen calls to him. His eyes flash toward her quickly and I take advantage, ripping out of his hold and running. I don't take the time to see if he's following me.

This time I'm shoving people out of my way. I don't care who it is, I just have to find him. People are yelling at me and pushing me back, but I keep going, my eyes scanning the crowd, looking for Craig. Finally, *finally* I have a reason to hit him. It pisses me off that it took him hurting Pris for it to happen.

He turns around a corner right as I approach the hallway. Without giving myself time to think, I lunge, shoving Craig into the wall.

"What the hell, Sinclair!" Right about that time, people start to step in around us, all itching for the fight that's about to go down. "I'd think you would be happy. Now that I dumped her, you'll have a chance." And then the prick *winks* at me.

I swing my arm and connect my fist with his jaw. It feels good. There's so much in my life I have no control over, but this? Protecting her? This is all mine.

Craig stumbles, tries to swing at me, but misses before I nail him again. My hand aches at the connection, but it doesn't matter. As soon as I go for a third, someone grabs me from behind. I know it's Sebastian without having to see him.

"Get the fuck *off*," I yell, but of course he doesn't. Then someone else is grabbing onto me and they're dragging me out of the house. A few people are around Craig, checking out his face as I fight to get back at him.

They toss me outside, whoever else helped him, heading back into the house and leaving only Sebastian and me on the porch.

"Fuck!" I don't remember ever being this pissed before. "Why'd you do that? You should have *helped* me!"

"Helped you what? Get the cops called on us? Upset Pris even more? Damn, Jay. You think I don't want to beat his ass just as bad as you do?"

"Ugh." I groan, reaching for my hat before realizing I must have lost it. I'm losing more than just that.

I wouldn't take it back, though.

"If that had been Aspen, you wouldn't have been pulling me off him." I turn and take the porch stairs two at a time. I'm on the street before I hear Sebastian's footsteps behind me.

"Low blow, man."

He's right, but I keep walking and he keeps following.

"Jay, I get it. Just chill out. Don't take off. I'll get the girls and we can bring them home and then head back to my place or something."

Yeah, like I can do that. She didn't want me there earlier, so I doubt she does now. My heart is still thudding. My breaths still quick and fast.

"Seriously. What's up with you, lately? You need to talk to me or whatever because right now you're looking like you're about to explode." He crosses his arms.

I don't have time to answer because his cell phone goes off. I'm still walking away and he's still following as he talks. A few seconds later, he says. "We gotta go back. The girls are waiting out front for us. Pris rode with Craig so she doesn't have her car."

Finally, I stop walking. "Go get them."

Bastian looks back down the street, then at me, and down toward the house again. "Come with me."

He's totally babysitting me right now and I don't like it. *"I can't do this with you, Jaden. Not with him here."*

"I can't go back or I won't be able to stop myself from looking for him," I say.

"Then wait. I'll grab them and be right back."

I tell him okay even though I don't plan to do it.

"Seriously, Jay. Don't bail."

"Then hurry up," I say, trying to sound light. As soon as he starts jogging back for the girls, I take off in the other direction.

CHAPTER THREE

I don't go home because:
1.) I hate the place. I never want to be there, but especially when I feel like this and
2.) I know Sebastian's determined ass is probably sitting in his car outside waiting for me. I'm not in the mood to see him or anyone else, so I walk around all night.

All.

Night.

Not my idea of a good time, especially since my hand is killing me, but I can't think of anything else to do.

The sun is just starting to come up when I walk through the front door of my house. The second I step inside, I hear Dad's heavy footsteps slamming against the hardwood floors. Great. He must have to work today. I turn to walk back out when he steps into the hallway.

"Are you just getting in, boy? Who do you think you are, coming into my house at this time of morning?"

His house, not mine, and I can't help but wonder when he's ever cared if I'm here or not. Or when I

26

come in, for that matter. "Won't happen again," I mumble because I'm not in the mood to deal with him.

Unfortunately, he seems to be in the mood to mess with me and by not playing his game, I probably just upped that need. When I try to walk around him, he grabs my arm. "So damn disrespectful. No matter what I do, you never learn any manners."

My brain files those words to the folder filled with everything else I've done wrong. "I said it won't happen again. Why don't you let me go?" I try to pull away, but he pulls me closer.

"Do I smell alcohol on you, little jerk?" His voice is harsh. Why does he hate me so much?

He doesn't give me time to answer before he rips his hand off me. "You're such a loser. You'll never amount to anything. Mooching off me and your friends, staying out all night and coming home drunk."

I'm going to explode. Like I'm a can of soda that keeps getting shaken, dropped, kicked, and finally I can't stop myself from exploding. After our last run-in, then Pris, walking around all night . . . I can't handle any of it anymore and I need to fight back.

"Jesus! You're like a broken record! Can't you come up with anything new? I know I'm a loser, you hate me, I'll never be anything. If you don't have anything new to throw into the ring, I'd like to go to my room now." I manage to take a few steps away from him.

His oversized face turns red. I see his jaw tighten. I've never, *ever* spoken to him like that.

I want to do it again.

"You little punk." For the first time in my life, his hand raises toward me. I brace myself for the blow, sort of glad it finally came to this.

Mom steps around the corner. "Mike . . . Don't, okay? Let's just go to the room and calm down." Her voice is shaking and I wonder if this will be the one thing to finally make her stand up to him. To finally worry about me.

"Did you hear the way he spoke to me? Of course you did. You always take his side. He's your little prize, isn't he? From when you thought you'd found something better, but it turned out I'm the only one who would put up with you."

Mom flinches at his words, her hand going to her face. I have no idea what he's talking about, but there's no way I'll let him speak to her that way.

"Leave her out of this. It's between you and me." An angered heat burns through me, threatening to turn me to ash, but I stand my ground. "You have something to say to me? Say it."

He suddenly laughs. It's a pissed-off laugh that makes my fists beg to hit him.

"Are you a big man now? About to graduate high school and you think you're a man?"

"Mike, no—"

He cuts her off. "Are you man enough to know your mom's a slut? How she screwed another man and got stuck with you? That I've been raising her little bastard kid for eighteen years because your real daddy didn't want you, either?"

I can't breathe. Each of his words are a fist, slamming into me. A foot kicking me.

Mom starts crying, hiding her face in her hands.

Dad? No, *Mike* is smiling.

I can't feel anything.

He's not my dad?

"That's right, kid. Your mom acted like a whore and then—"

His words are cut off when my fist rams into his face. I feel the bones crack, but I can't stop myself. I swing at him again. This time, he's ready for it. He knocks my hand away and shoves me into the wall. My hand slams against it. Pain shoots through my head, my knuckles, but it's nothing compared to the way my heart has been cut open.

Mom jumps between us, screaming, before he can

hit me again. Black makeup trails down her face with her tears. "Please, stop! Don't fight."

Mike looks over her at me. He's got a busted lip, but he smiles regardless.

"You're done for, kid."

Mom tries to stop him as he pulls out his cell phone and dials. I don't try to run. Probably couldn't move even if I wanted to. I slide down to the floor.

He's not even my dad.

And she still let him treat me this way.

The police ask me a million times what happened. Each time I admit to taking the first swing. What's the point in fighting it? They bring me to the hospital first. My hand is broken. Obviously punching two people in one night didn't agree with me.

Mom comes to the hospital, but I tell them I don't want her in the room and since I'm eighteen, they can't do anything about it. The police supervision is already enough of a downer.

She let someone who doesn't share my blood make my life hell.

I can't get over that.

Next I'm transferred to the police station. More supervision, like I'm some kind of criminal. I'm here for a few hours, telling them the same thing over and over. Yep, I hit him first. Yep, he defended himself.

A little while later, they tell me he's not pressing charges. I'm his son, after all. Yeah, right. Anyway, it's still getting sent to the DA's office for review. Apparently it's not only up to him what happens.

I'm sitting in the waiting-room chair when Mom runs in, pulling me into a hug.

I don't hug her back.

"Jaden! Why in the world would you talk to him like that? You know how he gets," she whispers as she sits next to me.

"Is it true?"

Her silence tells me it is. A million questions bear down on me. How? Who? Why? But I don't ask any of them.

"I called Courtney. I didn't tell her everything that's going on, but she said you're welcome to stay with Sebastian until you guys leave."

This makes my head whip around to face her. "You're kicking me out?" It's not like I want to go home anyway, but how can she do this? After everything, how can she choose him? How can she stay with a man who treats her, and her son, like garbage?

Her voice is even softer when she speaks again. "I don't think it would be a good idea to put you guys in the same house again. You're leaving in a couple weeks anyway . . . ."

And then, I have no idea where the words come

from. I'm angry and hurt, but I also don't want to be alone. I don't want to leave her with him. "Come with me. I don't have to go to New York. We can go anywhere."

She cocks her head, tears pooling in her eyes, and I know damn well she'd rather be there with him than anywhere with me.

The list of people who feel that way is piling up.

"Jaden . . . I love him. You're grown up. You have your life, and he's mine. I know it doesn't make sense, but he loves me, too. The things he said last night were only spoken out of anger. Things will be easier now . . . for both you and me. I want that for you."

She means things will be easier for her. She wants that for *her*. Her life with him will be better when I'm not around.

"What if he hurts you?" My voice actually cracks and it pisses me off.

"He won't."

Because the reminder of the one time he didn't have control over her will be gone?

"I don't know who I am without him, Jaden."

This is so far from funny, but I can't stop myself from laughing. "Maybe it's time you find out."

My words hit me. I'm not who I thought I was, either. I'm not Mike Sinclair's son; I'm just the bastard kid he hates. I haven't been Pris's best friend since last summer. Sebastian and Aspen don't need me following them around anymore either.

What do I know about myself? I'm the mooch, the loser, the guy who broke Pris's heart, the one she doesn't want to be there for her.

Yeah, totally not a prize winner. Not like I ever thought I was.

"I need you to do one thing for me, Mom. One thing and I'm gone."

I lie to Mom and tell her Sebastian is on his way to pick me up from the station, which actually could be true if she called Courtney. She hugs me, cries, playing the caring Mom routine pretty well. It can't be true, though. If she did care, she definitely wouldn't be choosing that asshole over me.

I plop back down into the ugly, brown chair. I have no idea what I'm going to do. I swear it can't be more than thirty seconds after she walks out that my eyes dart toward the door of the waiting room. Pris is standing about ten feet away from me. She's wearing a pair of pajama bottoms and a hoodie, although it's too hot to be wearing it. Her hair is tied back in a messy ponytail. Courtney must have told Sebastian what happened. He probably called Pris and she rolled right out of bed to come here.

I'm going to kill him.

With no other option, I push to my feet and walk over to her. "Hey . . ." The awkwardness between us is so screwed up. It's not supposed to be this way with my friends. It's the one thing I've always been able to count on.

"Hey . . . I got your hat. You dropped it when . . ."

Yeah . . . *When.* I still can't think about Craig without wanting to lose it. "Thanks." I take it from her.

"Bastian called to tell me you were here. We were all going to come get you, but I told him I wanted to do it alone." There's a question in her voice, wondering if it's okay that she's here. And it is. I didn't realize it until this second, but I'm glad it's her.

"Cool. Thanks."

Her eyes travel to my casted hand, to my face, and yeah, I know I'm screwed up. I look around, knowing how everyone else in this place sees me: wrinkled clothes from wearing them for two days, piercings, the whole nine. They're probably wondering what the hell the District Attorney's daughter is doing here with me. *Shit.* And he'll see the case, too. How bad does that suck?

"I can give you a ride to Sebastian's."

Yeah . . . yeah, I definitely need out of here. I want *her* out of here. Seconds ago I was glad it was her and now I feel guilty. Picking me up at the police station? Classy, right?

"Priscilla. Can you come here for a minute?"

Both our eyes snap to the side to see her dad standing there all suited up like he always is. He looks at my bruised face and busted-up hand totally different than Pris just did.

Yeah, I want to tell him. *I know I'm a mess and she deserves better.* That's the whole reason things are so screwed up between us. He says something to her in Spanish and she gives me a sad smile before saying she'll be right back.

"I'll wait outside." I don't look at them as I walk out so I can't see the disappointment on his face.

"You shouldn't have come," I tell her five minutes later as we're sitting in her car.

I know immediately by the way she tenses that I said the wrong thing. I'm almost grateful for it, because that's *us*. I say something stupid and she yells at me. It's the way we work and I like it, but instead of laying in on me like she's supposed to, her voice is soft when she says, "I was worried about you. Last night, I know you went after Craig for me and I don't know what happened at home, but . . . I don't know. I just wanted to be sure you're okay."

Now it's me who tenses. "I'm fine."

"You're stubborn," she counters. Her voice is getting a little louder and I can tell she's getting frustrated.

I want to hold onto this moment because it almost

feels like it used to. I don't want to focus on what happened this morning or last night or last summer. I just want this moment. "And sexy . . . Funny . . . Oh, and let's not forget I'm a good kisser."

The sides of her plump lips curve up a little. Pris shakes her head and mumbles, "*Stupido.*"

It's then I realize I'm smiling too.

We're quiet the rest of the ride to Sebastian's house. Pris doesn't kill the engine.

"Thanks for coming to get me or whatever."

Finally she turns to look at me. Her eyes are dark, such a dark brown you can hardly see her pupils. "Always. You know that, Jay."

And I do. No matter what, I know she'll be there.

"Are you okay?" Last night finds its way into my head again. "Because of . . . *Craig.*"

She reaches out like she's going to touch me, but then pulls her hand back. I've touched her a million times. Hugged her, had my arm around her, wrestled with her, but for some reason, I can't remember the last time it happened.

"You didn't have to fight him, Jay. It wasn't that big a deal. I was just hurt and embarrassed. It's not as if I really liked him that much anyway."

Then why were you with him? Why did you waste your time on him? "He's a loser. You're better off without him. You deserve someone way better than—yeah, I'm just . . ." I just have no clue what I'm saying. "Anyway, Sebastian's probably peeking out the blinds like an old lady right now. I better get in there."

I push open the door, but her words stall me from getting out. "If you won't talk to me, talk to him, okay? You don't have to be so strong all the time, Jaden."

Strong? No, not at all. I wink at her. "Girls dig strong guys."

I get out of the car and close the door behind me, not man enough to look back at her.

The second I hit the porch stairs, Sebastian is standing in the doorway.

"I hear I'm supposed to be staying with you to keep you under control for a while? Apparently, I'm your last resort." I hold out my fist, willing him to just bump it with his. To play my game and not ask any questions I don't want to answer right now.

But he doesn't.

Sebastian wraps an arm around my neck and pulls me inside. "Welcome home, man."

CHAPTER FOUR

The last couple weeks before school gets out go so slow, I seriously consider the idea someone learned how to alter time just to screw with me.

Sebastian keeps trying to get me to talk to him about what went down at home that night, but I just don't do the talking thing. I don't get how it's supposed to help. It's not going to change anything. Mike will still be a prick who hates me for Mom's screw-up, and I'll still be the son she never wanted who she let take the brunt of whatever happened between them.

No matter how many times I say it, those are the facts. Why put it out there so I can give them another reason to feel sorry for me? That's one thing I can't stand the thought of. Not when it comes to Sebastian, Pris, and Aspen.

Finally graduation day is here and Sebastian's leg is jumping up and down while the principal gives a year-long speech when all we want to do is throw our caps in the air and be done with it. Actually, that's not true. Sebastian's nervous and I'm nervous because, well . . . it's not like we can graduate without going out in style, right?

We've always known we wanted to do something big. Only we didn't know what it was until recently. At our school, you pick who you walk with and whatever order you get in for rehearsal, you're in for the ceremony.

I'm both on edge and excited as they get closer and closer to calling our names. Luckily, we have friends in high places (okay, maybe I mean people willing to be bought off) who agreed to help us.

Finally it's time for our row to stand up and walk to the stage. I give Sebastian a smile as we're waiting for our names.

"Sebastian Hawkins," the principal calls. "Jaden Sinclair."

As soon as my name clears his lips, the song, "I'm Sexy and I Know it" starts blasting through the speakers. The huge overhead screen on the stage flashes with the words, "Sebastian and Jaden Rock". The teachers scramble to figure out what's going on. But that's nothing compared to how the crowd starts roaring with laugher as we dance across the stage to our theme song.

Principal South comes after us, but we dance out of his reach.

We both do the pelvic thrust like in the video and the laughter grows.

Sebastian has a huge smile on his face. It only lasts about twenty seconds, but the moment is epic. For the first time in I don't even remember how long, I'm happy.

"Jaden!" Mom calls as I start to walk away from her. She didn't even mention anything about our graduation stunt. She hugged me, told me she loved me (yeah, right) and said everything was good for what I'd asked her to do for me.

"Yeah?" I turn back around to face her. It's so strange looking at her now. My whole life feels like a lie. Like I don't know who I am. Did I ever know? I'm not sure.

She holds out a paper. "Last summer, when things started to get worse with your father—"

"He's nothing to me." I grab the paper out of her hand.

"You're right . . . of course, but when things started to get worse, it's because he found out I had that." She points to the paper in my hand. "I thought you might want it someday."

Her brown eyes dart down. I should have known. How could I not have known? Neither she or Mike have blue eyes like I do.

For some reason I can't make myself look to see what's on the paper. Can't bring myself to say thanks, because I'm not even sure what I have to thank her for. "Bye, Mom," is all I say before I walk away. I hate walking away from her, but she did that first, right? Still, it makes me feel like a piece of shit.

I make my way over to Sebastian, Aspen, and their parents. Automatically my eyes scan for Pris, but she's not around.

"First of all!" Sebastian's mom, Courtney, grabs me and pulls me into a tight hug. "Good job and I'm proud of you."

"Thanks," I mumble into her hair as I return the hug.

She pulls away. "And second, I'll tell you just like I told him, what in the world were you boys thinking?"

Sebastian jumps in, "That we're sexy and we know it!"

We both start dancing. Aspen grabs ahold of him while Courtney and her husband Roger laugh. In between giggles she says, "I . . . don't . . . support . . . Oh, hell, it was pretty funny. You should have seen the look on your principal's face!"

It takes a good minute for all of us to stop laughing. Once we do, Courtney and Roger tell us goodbye and head for the packed parking lot.

"Where's Pris?" I ask. "Are we supposed to meet

her at the party or something?" Her parents are throwing her a huge party for her graduation. They actually offered to send her and Aspen somewhere, but Pris didn't want to go.

Aspen's eyes dart to Sebastian, who answers, "Nah, we're not going. I guess they wanted some family thing or whatever. We'll meet up with her later."

The ground suddenly becomes really interesting to them both. I'm about to ask what's up when it hits me. "They didn't want me there." It's not even a question because I know. I'm sure it would be pretty embarrassing for the DA to have the kid who was just at the police station all busted up, in his house and hanging out with his daughter.

As I walk away, I toss over my shoulder, "You guys go. I'll be cool." It's not like Pris's parents were ever really like Bastian's or Aspen's, but I'm pretty sure they never would have told Pris they didn't want me in their house before "the incident."

"Jay, wait up. They're assholes. They've always been too good for us." Sebastian comes after me.

"No." I turn to face him. "Not for us. For *me*. You guys are free to go, remember? I'm the only one they don't want around Pris." Which I'm pretty sure isn't anything new. I mean, yeah, they've always been civil to me, but I'm sure if Pris and I had gotten together, they would have blown their lids.

What is wrong with me? Why the hell does everyone have something against me?

"So go, have fun. We'll hang after or whatever." When I start to walk away again, Sebastian grabs my arm.

"Jay . . . Stop."

I don't know what it is about the way he says it, but I listen. I let out a deep breath.

"We're not going anywhere without you. You're my BFF." He cracks a smile and I can't help but do the same. Last summer I teased him about Aspen being his BFF and now he uses the saying all the time.

Even though I don't feel it, I try to return his lightness. "Whatever. Just don't expect me to paint your nails."

"You guys are so weird," Aspen pipes in, but then she leans her head on my shoulder. "We love you."

This is definitely becoming too much for me. "Shh, Bastian's not supposed to know about us, remember?" But all I can think about is they *are* going somewhere without me, they just don't know it yet.

When we pull up at Sebastian's house, Pris is sitting in her car. She definitely shouldn't be here right now. She's climbing out of her car, when I jump out of the Explorer. "What are you doing here?" I have a feeling, I know.

Pris shrugs. "The party wasn't really my thing. I made an appearance and left."

I groan. It sucks when my best friends feel like they have to babysit me. "Pris—"

She holds up her hand. "I didn't want to be there, okay? End of story. I don't want to fight with you about it, Jaden."

"Whatever."

We head into the house. Courtney and Roger are out so we pop some pizzas in the oven. Once they're done we head upstairs to Sebastian's room. It goes without saying none of us are in the mood to go out tonight—graduation or not.

The whole time we eat, my freaking gut is aching because I feel for the first time like I need to say something. Like I owe it to them. All this stuff seemed to pile on me at once and now I'm about to make an announcement. Like, relationship-altering stuff that I don't want to say, but now more than ever, know I have to.

"Dude, I seriously can't wait until we leave next week. I'm so ready to be out of this town. This road trip is going to be epic." Sebastian takes a bite of his pizza.

"What is with you and the word epic? Last summer was supposed to be epic, too." Aspen pushes him, but he grabs her and pulls her to his lap.

"Last summer *was* epic. You fell in love with me."

I try not to gag. On reflex, I look at Pris. Quickly, she turns away. The ache in my stomach multiplies. Why does everything always have to be so hard?

"Speaking of New York, I need to talk to you guys about that."

Three sets of eyes land on me and I wish I could take the words back. I bite my lip, pulling slightly on the ring there.

"Don't tell me you're going to say what I think you're going to say." Sebastian sits up straighter and Aspen moves off his lap.

I should have known he'd know. They probably all do. "I don't have all my shit figured out like you guys do. I'm not enrolled in school. I don't know what I want to do. It's not like I can tag along and mooch off you guys."

"Well, no shit. You'd get a job, just like the rest of us." Sebastian's voice is tight.

"Yeah . . . You're not the type to lie around. We all know that, Jay. You'd never try to mooch off anyone. Plus, you like electronics. You're always messing around with stuff . . ." Aspen tosses her opinion in.

Funny how it's the opposite of how I feel . . . of what Dad—I mean, Mike—thinks.

Pris doesn't say a word, and honestly, it might make

me a douche, but I don't have the balls to look at her.

"I just . . ." Don't know who I am . . . Where I belong . . . "It's not right, ya know? Everything is all screwed up right now—"

"More reason for you to get out of here!" Sebastian's eyes are wide, jaw clenched.

"I'm not staying here. I'm going to Texas. My mom's brother lives there. He's always been cool to me."

Pris pushes to her feet and runs out the door, leaving the rest of us sitting there with wide eyes. I immediately feel like shit. Without a thought, I'm going after her. She runs down the stairs, probably faster than I've ever seen her move.

After she rips it open, the door slams against the wall.

"Pris!"

She ignores me and keeps going. I don't catch up to her until she's trying to open the door to her car. Not knowing what else to do, I box her in, one arm on each side of her, my hands flat against the car. "I'm sorry." I have no idea what I'm apologizing for, but I need to say it. Actually, I do know. I'm sorry about it all: last summer, every month since then, and that I'm not who she deserves.

She doesn't turn around to face me, but her shoulders start to shake and I know she's crying.

"I'm sorry . . ." I tell her again, wishing I was man enough to tell her why.

That's when she whips around. Her eyes are swollen and red and I'm about to apologize again when she puts both hands on my chest and shoves. I stumble backward and she's going a million miles an hour, speaking in Spanish even though I have no clue what she's saying. She always talks in Spanish when she's mad or she's insulting someone. Right now, I know it's both.

"What are you sorry for, Jaden, huh? Why don't you tell me?" Her eyes are filled with fire. I don't know anyone who burns this brightly.

"I'm just sorry." I shrug. *Say it, Jay. Open your mouth and talk to her.*

"That's what I thought, Jaden. Whatever. Bail on us. Go to Texas. Do whatever you want."

I don't want to go to Texas. I want to go with them. Keep the plan. Hang out. Go to school. Be with her. *Say it.* "It's for the best."

"You should have told me."

"I just did."

She rolls her eyes. "You're right. I don't know what I was thinking. Why would I be different to you than anyone else?"

Pris's eyes start to water again and I flash back to the party on her birthday weekend last summer. I was hitting on a girl—I don't even remember her name. And we started kissing. Pris had been talking to the idiots they met at the pool hall, which made sense. She should have been with them and not me, but for some reason I pulled away. Pris wasn't with the guys anymore and I left to find her. She was sitting out back, her shoulders shaking like they just were and somehow I knew she was crying over me.

A real man would have gone to her. Wiped her tears. But I'd been too scared because I knew I couldn't be what she needed.

The second I turned to walk away, I knew she saw me, so I manned-up and headed for her. "What's up, Pris? Did someone mess with you?"

Yeah . . . me.

Quickly she'd wiped her eyes. Closer . . . I kept getting closer. . . . And closer . . . I don't know if it was the alcohol or what, but that was the moment everything started to get screwed up. We'd played it off, for a while after that, but I knew everything would be screwed up.

And I left her out there. I went inside and went to bed, ignoring the party downstairs.

I hated Craig for hurting her. I'd hate anyone for hurting her, which is just another reason to hate myself.

"I want to go with you—you guys, I mean. I want to go with you guys."

She stills, but then says, "Don't do me any favors."

I shake my head. "I'm not. I *want* to go. I *need* to go . . ." It's true. I need this trip with them. This last time to just be *us*. The way we were before everything got so messed up. "You know what? Forget Texas. We've planned this trip forever. Let's just do it. Let's go and have fun and like Bastian's dumbass says, it'll be epic."

"And then?" Her eyes are all soft and vulnerable. I don't know why she's asking because I can tell she knows.

The words want to stick in my mouth, but I find a way to push them out. "And then you'll go to NYU and you'll rock it, just like you do everything else." I take a deep breath. "And I'll be in Texas."

CHAPTER FIVE

The next couple weeks . . . well, they pretty much suck. Pris isn't around much. Sebastian keeps saying it's because her parents want to do all this stuff with her before she goes to New York, but I'm not that dumb. That might be part of it, but I know she's avoiding me. Not that I can blame her.

I haven't talked to Mom since graduation.

Honestly, I'm not sure how I feel about that, but whatever. It's not like I can change anything.

Apparently the DA isn't moving forward with charges, either. Like it really matters.

Finally it's the day after Pris's eighteenth birthday. The day we're leaving.

Sebastian's lame ass has been freaking out like he's hopped up on caffeine for two days straight. Last night, Courtney and Roger took us out for a goodbye dinner. Aspen's been with her parents and Pris with hers. And like I said, for me? Nothing.

It's five in the morning and Sebastian and I are sitting in his room. The girls are supposed to be here soon. I can't stop myself from wondering if Pris's parents know I'm going with them. They know Sebastian is, of course. They definitely made sure it would only be Aspen and Pris staying in the apartment they're renting. Oh, another thing for me to feel like shit about. How's Bastian supposed to afford a place without me?

"Can you believe we're finally doing this?" he asks, sitting on the edge of his bed. His leg is bouncing and he actually looks a little nervous.

"Don't tell me you're getting cold feet now. This is New York. You'll be out there with your girl and all that." This is always the way we've worked. I know out of anyone in the world, Sebastian would be the first one at my back, but we don't do that emotional stuff real often. One of us is always down to lighten the mood.

"Hell no. You know it's not that. It's just . . . We're, like, grown and shit now. I mean, our parents are helping with the apartments, but we're driving across the country by ourselves. Going to college. We have to find jobs. It's just . . . crazy."

His words hit me in the stomach because I won't be there. I was always supposed to be there. "It'll work out. You guys will love it." I push to my feet, feeling the pockets in my baggy shorts to make sure I have my wallet and the cell phone Courtney helped me get. I didn't want her help, but she said there's no way she'd let us drive across the country unless each of her boys had a phone. It makes me feel guilty.

"It won't be the same without you." Sebastian looks over at me. There's no joking in his face. It makes me want to get out of this room.

"Don't get all soft on me, Bastian. At least you won't have to worry about having a guy who's better looking than you around."

"First of all, you're nuts. I'm way hotter than you. And second, I'm being serious, man. We're like, Batman and Robin. Scooby and Shaggy. Actually, none of those duos have shit on us. We're *Sebastian and Jaden*. Who am I going to get to help me watch the girls? I mean, who else could pull off that 'I'm Sexy and I Know It,' dance, but us?"

He won't ask me to go. I know that, but this is almost as bad. It feels like crap, which is exactly the reason we don't usually do this mushy stuff. "You'll figure it out. Nothing holds Sebastian Hawkins down."

The look on his face tells me that's not what he wanted me to say. "Well, obviously. Not the same, though. Jay . . . What's going on with your parents? Don't let their shit get you down."

My head drops back and I groan. "This is all me, B, okay? It's just something I gotta do."

He shakes his head, but then he pushes to his feet. "Whatever. Then let's make a pact, right here. Let go of all that other shit on this trip. Your parents, you and Pris, and let's make this the most kick-ass road trip in history. Just like graduation, we're not getting out of here without doing it in style."

I hold out my fist and he hits it with his. "We're going to own this trip."

I'm leaning against Sebastian's Explorer while he says goodbye to his mom. Courtney's sobbing all over the place just like Aspen's parents are doing with her.

"You have the itinerary?" Courtney asks Sebastian.

"Yeah, Ma."

"And you know where you're staying every night, right?"

"Yeah, Ma."

"And you know you're supposed to call at least twice a day, remember. Once in the morning and once in the evening."

Sebastian doesn't answer, but pulls her into a hug. They're like that for an eternity before he pulls away and looks at Roger. "Take care of her, man. Remember, I'm only a phone call away. You hurt her, I'll—"

"You're a good son, Sebastian. I promise, I'll be good to her," Roger tells him before they shake hands.

The next thing I know, Courtney is standing in front of me. "I can't believe you boys are leaving me."

I try to smile at her, but I'm not sure I pull it off.

"I've known you since you were five years old, Jaden. I want you to know, you'll *always* be a son to me."

I can't help but compare her words to my mom's when she asked me to leave. I look toward the ground, about to try to say something stupid, but she grabs my face, so I'm looking at her. "I'm serious. *Always*, okay? You ever need anything, you get on that phone and call me. There is nothing I wouldn't do for you."

Her tight hug nearly takes the wind right out of me. I lean into it because, I might sound like a pussy, it feels good.

"I love you, kiddo," she whispers in my ear.

I swallow the golf ball in my throat. "Yeah . . . I love you too."

The car is silent as we pull away. Aspen will see her parents in a few weeks when they come out, but I'm not sure about the rest of them. Pris's parents are always going somewhere so I'm sure she'll see them a lot, too, but you can tell, it's still a big deal.

Sebastian is driving and Aspen's up front with him. Priscilla is stiff, sitting as far away from me as she can. She's got on a pair of shorts. Her legs are killer. Always have been. All curvy and creamy brown. I shift in my seat. Yeah, this is definitely going to be a long trip.

"You okay?" I ask her. Her only reply is a nod.

The quiet thing is going to make things even worse.

After about forty-five minutes into our drive through Southern Oregon, Sebastian pipes up. "Okay, this drive is way too low key. We're free. Do you guys realize how cool that is?"

"I'm sure you'll inform us," Aspen says and that's all it takes for the two of them to get going.

I look over at Pris to make commentary about them, but it's like she's on the other side of the continent or something. Yeah, this is my fault and I get it, but I hate it, too. I want to tell her something, find a way to pull her back to me so we can be like we always have been—the four of us, but is that an asshole thing to do since things aren't the way they used to be? I don't know.

"Let's do something. Who wants to play I Spy?" Sebastian asks.

I thump him in the back of the head. "Are you five?"

"I don't see you throwing out any suggestions so stop trying to ruin my fun."

"Okay then, what about the fact that once you see something, we're past it? How are the rest of us ever supposed to guess?"

"He has a point there, Bastian," Aspen says. This is where Pris would usually have something to say, too. She's good at those smart comments, but she still hasn't said a word.

"Hey, you're supposed to have my side!" Bastian tells her.

Aspen laughs. "Only when you're right."

I nudge Pris's leg. "What do you think we should do?"

"I don't know." Pris pulls out her iPod and puts the buds in her ears. Oh-kay. Guess she really doesn't want to talk to me.

She listens to music while Sebastian, Aspen, and I keep talking. We go through a few CDs, this and that, and she's still being all quiet and I swear it makes me feel like I'm going to explode. I can't stop myself from playing with the piece of paper in my pocket. I've had it with me ever since Mom gave it to me at the graduation. I've looked at it a million times, but haven't done anything about it. What a surprise, huh?

We stop for lunch. Afterward, Bastian and I decide to switch up so I can drive a bit. Pris and Aspen are over by the diner and I can tell Pris is pissed. Whatever's going on she's about to blow her lid, and finally she stomps back over to the SUV, jumps into the front seat and slams the door.

"Shit," I groan, and Sebastian shrugs as if to say he

doesn't know what her problem is. I do. It's me. Yeah, I don't even have to say that doesn't feel good.

About fifteen minutes into me driving, Sebastian and Aspen pass out in the back seat. They're all cuddled up together and this is where I'd usually blurt out something stupid to make fun of him. I kind of want to, but it doesn't feel right anymore because where he's sitting is definitely better than where I am.

"You wanna listen to anything specific?" I ask, flipping through the CD case while I drive. The GPS on the dash is telling me where to go.

"No."

My eyes dart to hers, which makes me sort of run off the road a little. Nothing major.

"Jaden! Watch where you're going!" She rolls her eyes at me.

Take a deep breath. Chill out. I'm trying to remind myself she's not usually like this. That she's still pissed at me because of way too many things to count, but this isn't what I wanted. This isn't the way this trip is supposed to go.

Instead of saying anything, I just keep driving. Eventually she falls asleep and everyone in the dumb car is out cold except for me.

Unfortunately, there's not even anything interesting

to look at. The road trip idea is cool and all, but there isn't much to look at along this route we chose. We have some stuff planned for Salt Lake and Chicago, but that's about it.

A soft snore comes out of Pris and I can't stop myself from laughing. I'll definitely have to give her crap about that one. But then I remember I can't. The old Pris and Jaden could have done that. How did things get so screwed up? Oh yeah. Me.

Somehow I feel the weight of the paper in my pocket. Can't stop myself from wondering if I'll ever use it when I know I won't.

After driving for a few hours, I really have to go to the bathroom so I pull into a gas station, pulling up to the pumps.

"Wake up, pretty boy." I throw an empty, balled-up bag of chips at Bastian. "I have to take a piss. I'll pay to fill it up while we're here."

He reaches for his wallet, still looking half asleep. "You don't have to pay. I got it."

Instead of replying, I shake my head and get out of the car. Now I can't even pay for gas? "You want anything, Priscilla?" I'm standing by the driver side door, looking at her. It takes me a minute to realize what I called her. No one ever calls her that, but yeah . . . it fits her. Different and kind of exotic like her. I let it slip once in a while, but that's it. That's why it pissed me off so much when Craig used the name.

She shakes her head and then scrambles out of the passenger side. By then Aspen is climbing out and they do the typical girl-bathroom thing where they go together and do who knows what in there.

"What's her problem?"

Bastian looks at me like I just asked the dumbest question in the world.

"Seriously. She's the one who wanted me to come and she won't even say a word to me."

Then he shakes his head like he's disappointed in me, which really annoys me because I didn't do anything. I'm just trying to live my life and do what I have to do.

Keep lying to yourself there, Jaden.

"Come on. Let's gas up."

I've gone in, done my business, paid for gas, and bought myself a Cherry Pepsi by the time everyone piles back into the car. Suddenly, I'm wishing I had gotten a snack. Next to me, Pris is eating Cheetos, which she knows I love, and she's licking the cheese off her fingers, which I also love.

Seriously. It might not sound hot, but it is. It might be because it's her. I don't know, but it's hard not to offer her my help. How is it girls can make the smallest things sexy and not even know it? Her nails are painted this bright red that probably looks even brighter because her dark skin. Her tongue sneaks out of her mouth and—

Hooooonk!

"Holy shit!" I jerk the steering wheel as the Explorer veers into the next lane and almost into another car.

"Jaden!" Pris screams.

"Dude! Watch my car!" Sebastian yells from the backseat.

"What was that?" Aspen asks.

I'm pushing my hair out of my eyes like that was the problem when really it was Pris and her tongue. "Nothing. No biggie."

"This is the second time you've almost killed us!" Pris is using that pissed-off voice that she's pretty much speaking with 24/7 now.

"Chill. It was an accident. Nothing happened."

"Whatever." She crosses her arms, putting an end to the show that almost made me wreck.

Aspen reaches up and sort of massages her shoulder like Pris needs support or something. I glance in the rearview mirror and see Bastian shake his head like he's getting frustrated.

That makes two of us, bro.

I can't stop wondering if I shouldn't have come at all.

About an hour and a half later, Aspen and Sebastian are sharing an iPod, one of the buds in her ear and the other in his. They were messing with the portable DVD player earlier, but something's up with it, so I guess they resorted to this.

Pris hasn't spoken a word to me since her "whatever" earlier, but I have no idea what to do about it. Why do girls have to be so confusing? I mean, if this was Bastian he'd open his mouth and tell me what's up, we'd hash it out and be done with it. Usually that's the way Pris would be too, but everything's so different now.

I want things to go back to the way they were before.

Pre-Jaden running and pre-Pris thinking she liked me.

Without thinking, I reach over and stick my hand into the bag of Cheetos on her lap and grab a handful. Pris mumbles something under her breath. I almost ignore her, but I'm tired of playing this game. There's no point in us being here if we're going to fight the whole time. "What?"

"Nothing."

"No, I'm pretty sure you said something. Unless I'm hearing things. I don't think I'm hearing things."

She jerks her head to the left to look at me. "I said *help yourself.*"

"Dude! Chill out. You're like Godzilla on hormones lately."

"*Dios!*"

The Spanish starts rolling off her tongue and I know she's pissed, but so what. *Dios* is one of the only words I know and it means, "God." She's definitely not saying it the praising way.

I'm pissed too, though. I open my mouth to say something, but Sebastian beats me to it. "That's it. Pull the hell over."

"What?" I ask.

"Get off the freeway. There's an off-ramp."

"The more we stop, the longer it's going to take to get to Salt Lake." It's twelve hours from home, but that's where we wanted to make it the first day and then to spend some time there.

"Dude, get off. I'm serious. We're not going to Salt Lake."

I groan, but hit the ramp to get off the freeway.

"There's a Best Western over there. Pull in, we're done. Seriously, you guys are giving me a headache."

Unlike me, Pris has Aspen's support as she's leaning toward Pris, with her hand on her shoulder.

I pull up in front of the hotel, about ready to walk away from all of them.

"Woodstock, can you get us a room?" Bastian asks her all sweet and sucking up.

Pris is already jumping out of the car and slamming the door.

Really?

"Sure. Where are you guys going?" she asks him.

"We'll be back in a bit. Jay and I are going for a little ride."

CHAPTER SIX

"**S**coot over," Sebastian tells me, and I climb into the passenger seat.

"Sir, yes, Sir!" I salute him, but he ignores me and jumps behind the wheel before pulling away. He's in one of his pissed-off Bastian moods so I know we're about to get into it.

He doesn't say anything as he drives. I see a sign that says we're in Elko, wherever that is. All I know is it's not Salt Lake and that's where we're supposed to be spending our first night. Finally, after he keeps driving, obviously not knowing where we're going, I blurt, "Just say it. I swear, sometimes you're more of a drama queen than a six-year-old girl."

This gets his attention quickly. "I'm a drama queen? What do you call whatever's going on between you and Pris? Seriously. You guys are screwing with my mood. I feel like I need to call Daddy Peace for some lessons on meditation or some shit."

"I could always knock you out if that would be easier. I know it would be for me."

He just looks at me and shakes his head. "Oh! Arcade." Bastian makes a quick turn and parks.

"We stopped four hours early and left the girls to play video games?"

"Obviously." Sebastian jumps out of the car and I follow. I don't know if he thinks I'm an idiot or what, but at least I'll score a few games out of it.

We head inside to all the flashing lights and loud sounds. After getting quarters we play a few games before we grab a drink and sit down in one of the booths. It reminds me of the place back home we used to hang out at, only this place is actually bigger. My drink is about halfway done when I'm tired of playing his game. "So what's up? You decide to play counselor today or what?" I slouch back in the seat. My hair flops down in my face and I push it away before biting at the hoop in my bottom lip.

Sebastian looks way more serious than I need him to look right now. What I want is for him to make some smart-aleck comment and for me to counter it with something else.

After what feels like . . . I don't know, a long time, he says, "Things are changing."

Yeah, no crap. "Things always change." I shrug.

"Not the four of us. We're not supposed to change."

I let my head rest against the back of the booth and close my eyes. I totally don't feel like doing this right now. A lot of people think Bastian's all talk—that he doesn't take things seriously or that he doesn't really think about anyone but himself. Those people don't know anything. He's seen a lot—had a lot of people come in and out of his life and the one thing he's always serious about is holding onto the people he doesn't want to lose. I feel like shit that I'm pulling out the serious Sebastian.

I don't open my eyes when I say, "My head's all screwed up right now."

"Then tell me why."

"I can't."

"Then find a way to get it together yourself."

This makes me open my eyes. I know he's right, but it's not like I can snap my fingers and forget every single word that's been embedded into my brain. Can't forget that I'm a screw-up. That Mom obviously couldn't care less and . . . surprise! I don't even know who my real dad is. It's embarrassing, and I don't want everyone feeling sorry for me. "It's not that easy."

Sebastian groans. "Then talk to someone or whatever. I don't know. If you don't wanna tell me, talk to Pris or Aspen or something, but—"

"Pfft. You have said so yourself, Pris has always wished I would die a fiery death and I'm pretty sure things are double as bad now."

"Nah . . . I used to think that was it, but it's more than that and you and I both know it, man."

I don't answer him, not sure how I really feel about what he says. It's easier to pretend things don't exist than to talk about them and make them real.

"Whatever's going on, you need to find a way to squash it, because we can't keep going how we are. Last summer, it felt like shit when everything went down and none of you guys were talking to me. Now your dumbass is going all the way to Texas. Do you really want to be out there knowing you left things like this?"

He's right. I know that and I feel like we keep going over and over the same thing. My fault? Yep, and I definitely don't think I can keep going the way things are going right now. It's not fair to Pris. To any of them, actually. For once, I just want us to *be*. Simple. Without complications. I want to have fun and everything to be cool, before things change in the exact way Bastian is talking about.

I start to laugh. Sebastian looks at me like I just lost it and maybe he's right.

"What?"

"You actually make sense now! After always thinking you know what you're talking about, you actually might now. It's scary as hell."

Sebastian flips me off. "Whatever. I've always known my shit."

That makes one of us.

We hang out at the arcade a little longer before heading back to the hotel. Bastian texts Aspen to find out our room number. When we get up there, the girls are sitting in the middle of one of the beds, painting their toenails. My first thought is I sure hope they don't expect me to share a bed with Sebastian. He's my boy and all, but there's no way I plan to stay in the same bed as him all night.

Which is probably the stupidest thought I could have. Like he won't want to sleep with Aspen. But then that leaves me with . . . yeah. I'm totally going to die on this trip.

"Took you guys long enough. We're starving." Aspen gives us a look that says Bastian is totally in trouble. I look at Pris, the idiot in me wondering if I'll see the same look, but she's staring at her feet.

"Wanna go grab something, baby?" Bastian asks her.

"Yeah." Aspen starts walking toward him all funny, I'm guessing because of her wet toenails. "And I'm thinking I deserve an ice cream too. Come on, Pris."

Pris looks up for the first time since we walked in.

Her dark eyes skate over me quickly before landing on Aspen and Bastian. "I'm okay, actually. I'm kind of tired. I think I'll stay."

I jerk forward as something hits me in the back. After catching my balance I turn toward Sebastian and give him a dirty look. Yeah, like I need him to elbow me to clue me in that I should be staying too. "Umm . . . yeah. Me too."

Half of me expects Pris to suddenly get really hungry, but she doesn't. She just starts painting her nails again.

"We'll bring you guys back something in case." They're already walking toward the door. Before they go out, Sebastian adds, "Don't do anything I would do." Then, laughing, he slams the door behind them.

Idiot.

"Wha'cha doing?" I ask her.

Her eyebrows rise. Yeah, dumb question. I get it. I'm actually sort of freaking out; I don't know what to say to her. I don't like it, not only because I should know what to say to a girl, but I should know what to say to *this* girl.

"You want to go for a walk or something?"

She looks up at me and it's almost as though she's trying to tell me something with the look, I have no idea what it is. I'm positive she's going to say no, when she shrugs and mumbles, "Sure."

Slowly she gets up and slips her feet into a pair of flip-flops. She grabs the key card and slips it into the back pocket of her shorts and, again, she has me wishing to be something I've never wanted to be before. At this moment, that key card is the luckiest thing in the world.

The street in front of the hotel is packed with businesses and shops. Cars pass every few seconds. Definitely not the best place to talk. We stand out here for a few seconds and I already realize this was a stupid idea. It may be after seven now, but we're also in Nevada and it's *hot*.

Looking around, I see there's a pool around back and head that way. We go around the corner and for once I get lucky because no one is there.

"Come on." I nod my head toward the pool and she follows me over.

I open the gate and she walks in. Priscilla heads over to the far corner and I follow her.

"It's hot. We can go back to the room if you want to."

"I'm good if you're good." Still no eye contact from her.

"I'm good, too. We can put our feet in." But then I remember her nails. "That might mess up your nails or whatever though. We could go back to the room," I say again. "We should have stayed in the room."

Pris slips out of her shoes, sits down, and puts her feet in the water.

"Come on, pretty boy. Don't tell me you're afraid of messing up your nails?" For the first time in forever, she sort of smiles at me. And yeah, it might sound stupid, but I missed it.

"Yeah, right. Sebastian's the one you have to worry about for stuff like that." I step out of my Vans, pull off my socks and sit next to her. I roll my baggie shorts up so they're above my knees and watch as Pris's leg makes circles in the water.

After who knows how many circles, I get the balls to speak. "So . . . things have been kind of weird for a while."

Priscilla actually laughs. "Weird? Yeah, you can say that. I think it has to do with the fact that I was in love with you, thought you might feel the same, almost kissed you, got my heart broken, thought I got over you, only to get broken again when I found out you're leaving."

Oh, damn. I start to choke. On what, I don't know, but I'm coughing and trying to catch my breath like an idiot when I shouldn't be surprised. This is *Pris* and she doesn't hold back. But still, we've never talked about the almost-kiss at the beach house. She's never said anything like this to me before and damn if it isn't hot. Not that I should think that, but I do.

71

She starts to pound on my back. "Come on, pretty boy. Breathe. Let's not pretend you didn't know."

Once I'm able to stop acting like a psychopath, I look at her. Take in her slightly round face, plump lips, and for the first time in what feels like forever, I feel like she's really looking at me too. "I thought you hated me now."

There's a part of me who wants to be put out of my misery at my words. I thought you hated me now? How needy can I sound? But there's another part of me who needs to know. Who might just be as needy as I sound. I'm not proud of that part. I actually want to lock it deep inside and forget it's there, kind of like how my dad may have forgotten about me. Does he even know about me? Oh, that's right. Mike said he didn't want me.

Priscilla sighs. It's crazy because she's always so fierce. So strong that it makes me feel like crap that I may have dented her armor.

"I think I did . . . do . . . no. I did, a little bit. I'm not going to pretend I'm not angry or hurt. But I'm also tired of it too. Bastian's right. It shouldn't be like this. I don't want to fight with you anymore, Jaden."

"We're good at fighting." I wink at her.

"Oh, I know. I still think you're in *idiota*, but I'm tired of being mad at you. I'm tired of being hurt."

"Shit," I groan, rubbing a hand over my face. "You're the last person I want to hurt, Priscilla."

"I know that."

More circles with her feet. They look wobbly through the water. I can't help myself from thinking about how strong she is. Her leg looks unstable under the water, like it's made of Jell-o or something, but this is part of Priscilla which means it's sturdy . . . unbreakable. How kick ass is this girl? She's probably the strongest person I know.

"That doesn't make it any less real though," she says. "I guess it wasn't all your fault, either. You can't help how you feel. Or don't feel, for that matter."

I do feel it. I shouldn't, but I do.

"No," I shake my head. "It's my fault. After we almost kissed last summer I kind of . . . I don't know, freaked or something. I know it was the alcohol or whatever, but I could have handled it better . . . Should have handled it better."

It had been so crazy, standing behind that house with her. I'd found a way to wipe her tears. Neither of us spoke and then we were just heading toward each other. Like fucking beacons or something, we were pulled together. I got so close. I smelled her breath and felt its heat on my lips and then it was over. I realized what was going on and I pulled back.

And of course, the next day we blamed it on drinking. And the rest of the trip we got along like we had in forever, but yeah. Things changed when we got home. I realized how I'd almost screwed up and the next thing I knew, I kept pulling farther and farther way.

"That doesn't really matter, Jay. The fact is, I know when to let things go, and I have to. I'm moving on. I just want . . ."

For a minute I'm not sure if she drifted off or if I just stopped hearing. If somehow my hearing cut out when she said she's moving on from me. I want to tell her that she can't. She's mine. In a way we've always belonged to each other. Since that hair pulling incident in kindergarten our lives have been so intertwined: Me, Priscilla, Bastian and Aspen, but now she's moving on. And they've moved on. It's like everyone is moving on—going toward something, and I keep slipping farther behind. "I don't want to lose you," I blurt out.

"You'll never lose us, Jay. What is it you guys always say? We're a package deal or whatever? I just want to get back to what we were. I want to be cool, you know? I don't want to have to yell at you for eating my chips or to ignore you."

For some reason, I fight to find my voice. It's like it's locked in that piece of me I wanted to hide earlier.

74

Everything feels all wrong, but I can't say why. Instead, when I open my mouth, the words, "They're Cheetos. Not chips," fall out.

Priscilla shakes her head. "*Stupido.*"

Does it make me a nutcase that I miss her calling me that? "Drama Queen."

She doesn't reply so we sit there in silence, her feet dancing in the water. The sun is starting to go down now. Like a red fireball being extinguished by the desert. Finally, I nudge her with my elbow. "So, a truce, huh?"

"Yeah. A truce." And then, "I'm going to miss you when you go to Texas. I really want the next few days to be perfect."

I turn to look at her; a piece of her dark hair is now flying in the slight breeze, moving around like her legs are in the water. And man do I want to kiss her and touch her. Memorize her with my hands. "I'm going to miss you, too."

I can't make myself tell her even if the next few days aren't perfect, this moment is.

"So, who are you staying with in Texas?"

"My uncle. He's—"

"He helped you get the beater, right?"

"Yeah." I smile. Damn, I'm getting soft. I don't even know why I'm smiling right now. "He owns a junkyard." I shake my head, because . . . well, that sort of sounds ghetto. I'm talking to this gorgeous, rich girl with a District Attorney for a dad and I'm talking about going to live at a junkyard?

I don't know what makes me do it—maybe it's to change the subject or maybe it's because it's something I would have done before, without a thought, or maybe I just want an excuse to touch her, but something makes me grab her. My arms slip around her before I push off the concrete and throw us both in the water.

Surprised, Pris goes easily when I pull us under. It's only a second before she's twisting and turning and just like she should be, she's out of my grasp.

When I break the surface, I shake my head, water spraying all over the place. At first, her eyes are narrow and I know I'm in trouble, but then a wave of water flies and hits me in the face.

"That's it. You're going down, Mendoza." I push more water at her. We go back and forth, laughing the way we used to before everything got screwed up. It's cool because she's happy and she's smiling, and damn it feels good to be the one to make her feel that way. I just want to keep it going.

Later, we're still laughing as we stumble into the hotel room, soaking wet. Aspen and Bastian are laying on one of the beds.

"What the hell happened to you guys?" he asks.

Our clothes are obviously soaking wet and we're dripping on the carpet. They have the AC on so it's cold as hell, but neither of us cares.

I look at Pris and she's looking at me and I know we're thinking the same thing. Both of us fly at Bastian and Aspen. As they try and pull away, yelling, Pris and I soak them, and I start to feel like my family is back together again.

CHAPTER SEVEN

Early the next morning, I'm sitting in the car waiting for the other three to come down. My eyes are a little scratchy because I didn't sleep too well. First of all, how was I supposed to actually sleep with Priscilla in the same bed? I mean, *come on.* I'm a guy and she's a girl and she's right there and my body definitely knows it. She made these little sounds through the night and each of them hit me like little pinpricks in my body.

Then she'd roll over; her leg would kick out or her arm would come toward me. Yeah, totally not going to let you know how some of that stuff affected me.

Then when I'd finally fall asleep . . . she'd snore. It's not as bad as Aspen made it sound and I know that's not really supposed to be a big turn on or anything, but yeah, it was, okay. It's cool she feels comfortable enough around me to sleep and not worry about it.

Still, I'm tired as hell today and glad we're not going to be driving too long. We decided to keep with the original plan to stay in Salt Lake even though we're a day late getting there. That will give us some more time to hang out and have some fun.

It wasn't very easy for the others to explain to their parents why we didn't go there last night, but it all worked out.

Bastian and I have already loaded the car with the stuff and he ran to see what is taking the girls so long.

I lean my head back, playing with the keys while I wait for them to get down here. A few minutes later, Bastian jumps in the back beside me. Aspen's taking the first driving shift today.

"They're on their way," he tells me. There are a few minutes of silence which when it comes to Bastian, I know it can't be a good thing. When he speaks again, he confirms it. "So . . . about you and Pris."

I can't help it, I start to laugh.

"What's so funny?" He pouts like he's famous for.

"You. Aren't you the one who's always saying not to ask about other girls?" He used to give me crap when I asked him about some girl he was hooking up with or whatever. Not that Priscilla and I are doing that, but still. I have to take my shots against him where I can.

"That's different. This is one of our girls."

His words make my stomach hurt. They shouldn't

79

because she *is* just as much his girl as she is mine. They're good friends just like we are, but it makes me feel like puking. "There's nothing to tell, Gossip Girl. We talked. We're cool and that's that."

Luckily, I see the girls coming to save me from Sebastian and anymore questions I don't want to answer. They head to the back of the Explorer and I get an idea. I elbow Bastian who looks at me funny, but waits to see what I'm going to do. We keep facing the front. Once they finish getting whatever they needed, I hear the rear door close, I hit the button to make it pop open. One of the girls grabs it and closes it again. The second it clicks, I hit the open button again.

"What the heck?" I hear Aspen say. I can see Bastian biting his cheek so he doesn't laugh.

"Do it hard. Maybe you have to slam it?" Priscilla replies to her.

This time they slam it so hard, it practically vibrates the Explorer and my finger jabs the button making it pop open again.

"Jaden!" Priscilla shrieks. "You dork!"

By now Bastian and I are rolling in the backseat we're laughing so hard. I have no idea how she knew it was me and not him, but it's funny as hell.

"Do it hard!" I toss back at her which makes Bastian start to laugh even louder.

Priscilla gives me a dirty look when she climbs into the passenger seat, but I can see a smile trying to peek through. "You need serious help."

"Are you kidding? That was classic."

"You guys totally have to listen to our music for that."

"And close the hatch!" Aspen adds.

Still laughing, I get out and close the back door before tossing the keys to Aspen. A few minutes later, we pull onto the street and a harmonica comes through the speaker before some guy starts singing, his voice kind of gravely, but somehow smooth at the same time.

"Umm, what the hell is this?"

"Our music. It's Bobby Long." Priscilla doesn't even look back when she replies.

"Bobby who?"

"You heard me."

"Argh. We're in for a long few hours, man," Bastian says from beside me.

"Word."

By the time Aspen pulls onto the freeway, it cuts into another song about some chick wearing green, pink, and all these colors. I totally don't get what the guy is talking about, but even though I won't admit it, it might not be so bad. As the guy keeps singing, I let my eyes close to get some sleep, thinking about

Priscilla's smirk and how I know she thought my joke was funny too.

"Jay, wake up. Are you hungry?"

Clouds are trying to part in my head at the sound of Priscilla's voice. Man, I must have really passed out. My eyes open and she's standing at my open door, Bastian and Aspen nowhere in sight.

"We stopped to eat. You want something?"

"Yeah. I'm starved." We didn't eat breakfast before we left this morning and my stomach is growling.

They stopped at some hole-in-the-wall diner that looks like it came out of a movie or something, I'm assuming because we're in the boonies and there's nowhere else to go.

Priscilla scoots back and I get out of the car and stretch, before walking with her. Once we get inside I realize I really need to take a leak. My mouth is all dry and cottony, too. Priscilla starts to head over to Bastian and Aspen who are sitting in a corner booth, when I stop her. "I'm going to the bathroom. If they take a drink order before I get back, will you grab me a soda?"

"I guess." She winks at me and I freeze, because damn it's hot when a girl winks.

I do my business and then wash my hands and splash some water on my face, hoping it will help

82

me wake up. When I'm done, I'm walking back to the table when I see Priscilla halfway across the room from our table, with the waitress. It looks like she had to run to catch up with her or something.

"Umm, excuse me. I was on the phone and my friend accidentally ordered a Pepsi for my other friend, but he likes Cherry Pepsi. Is it too late to change that?"

I start to step around the corner to tell her it's not a big deal. I like Cherry Pepsi better, but I can drink anything. But it kind of is a big deal. Which, yeah, I know. It's lame. Who cares what kind of soda it is, but that's not the point. What matters is she knows what I prefer. That she left the table to talk to the waitress so I would have the kind of freaking soda I want. Not because she had to or because I asked for a specific kind or any of the other billion reasons someone can do something they're obligated for. She just did it . . . for me. Just because she wants me to have what I like.

Yeah. To me, that totally is a big deal.

So I stay ducked around the corner and let her finish talking to the waitress and then I watch her head back over to the table and sit down before I head that way, too. Plopping down beside her in the booth, I look around the table and say, "Please tell me one of you were smart enough to get me a Cherry Pepsi."

"Umm, yeah. I did." Priscilla almost looks embarrassed.

Me? I feel good, because even though I didn't come out and say it, I found a way to thank her for thinking of me. Sometimes it's easier to say things when you don't really have to say them at all.

Honestly? We don't really have a ton of stuff planned in Salt Lake. There are two things we really want to do. Sebastian is determined to go rafting down the Provo River. He thinks it will earn him man points or something—not that the rapids are too huge or anything, but we've heard it's a good time.

The other thing is we're supposed to eat at this place called café Rio. Priscilla and her family eat there when they come to stay at the place they keep here for when they coming skiing in the winter. Yep, she has a place in Salt Lake. Which, in the grand scheme of things, isn't that big a deal, but also, she has a second house in Salt Lake. And we're staying there. Should be a good time, right?

Back to the café. According to her, they make their own tortillas on a stone or something. Sounds strange to me, but she says it's the best place to eat Mexican food while you're here.

Once we get into town we head to the house first. It's seriously huge. Probably three of my houses. It's never really bothered me because she's not one of those girls who flaunts it. Priscilla couldn't honestly give a shit about her parents' money, but since I've been on a poor-me-kick lately, it kind of sucks. I keep thinking about how her dad looked at me at the police station all beat up and pierced and then the fact that they obviously didn't want me at her graduation party and suddenly Mike's words start trying to push their way into my head again. Into our trip when I don't want that bastard anywhere near us.

Not that I'm not a bastard too.

The elbow that's holding my head up gets pushed out from under me, snapping me out of it. I turn and Priscilla is sitting by me. She starts mumbling stuff in Spanish.

"Why do you do that when you know I have no clue what you're saying?" I sound pissy now even though I know I shouldn't.

She and I are in the kitchen and I'm not sure where the others snuck away to. I'm pretty sure they're locked in a room and we won't want to bother them, though.

"I do it because I don't want you to know what I'm saying. Or when you make me mad." She shrugs. "Or as it typically goes, both at the same time."

She's wearing this little tank-top thing that shows a whole lot of skin. I'm not sure if I want to thank

God or pry my eyes out because it sucks to be able to see and not touch.

"What did I do?"

"*Dios,*" she sounds frustrated now. Priscilla leans over the counter that separates us. Her head is in her hands, her elbows on the counter the way I just was. "Because you're getting upset, or thinking about something you don't like. Or something that bothers you, that you'll pretend isn't a big deal and never tell us, because why would Jaden need his friends?"

For a second, I'm stunned. I want to tell her I'm not like that, but we both know I am. Then I want to find out if she's freaking psychic, because how else would she know what I was thinking? And, third, let's get back to the stunned part because Priscilla has never really been one to keep things in, but first her admission last night and now this? She's usually not *quite* so open. I'm not sure what to think of it.

"I need you guys," is what comes out of my mouth. *I need you guys?* Could I sound any more like a douche?

"Okay." She shrugs and then grabs a glass out of the cabinet, before filling it with water.

Leave it alone, Jay. She's letting you off the hook. Instead, my word vomit continues when I ask, "What do you mean, okay? That means you don't believe me." Holy shit, do I sound like a girl right now. What's wrong with me?

She sighs and I want to do the same thing. I have no idea how we got on this road anymore and I'm definitely not sure if I want to keep traveling it or get the hell off.

"What were you thinking about, Jaden?"

How my dad isn't my dad. That he's told me all my life I'm a piece of shit. Oh, and you're the opposite of that. "Nothing."

She shakes her head. "Point proven. One for me, zero for you. I know you need us, but I also know you'll never let me be there for you. You'll never admit anything to me—I mean, us. I'm tired of pretending otherwise."

I groan, really not in the mood to do this. "Can we let it go? You never showed me what room I'm staying in."

Another head shake. And, yeah, another point for her.

I'm lying in Pris's bed. Alone. Which totally sucks, but whatever. She's staying in her parents' room while the newlyweds take the spare room. I'm sure they're enjoying the alone time.

I play with my cell phone, letting it roll around in my hand. To call or not to call? Okay, that was lame and, yeah, of course I'm going to call because I'm obviously a glutton for punishment. I mean, Mom pretty much made it clear she didn't care when she kicked me out, but the head and the heart? They don't always use the same frequency. I think mine has a particularly bad connection.

There's a part of me that doesn't want to talk to her, or wants to think I don't. I'm not sure which, but she told me to go and I went, ready to walk away, but, yeah, totally not as easy as I thought.

A few more minutes pass as I wait for it to ring. I don't know why. It won't. Not unless it's Sebastian from the other room being lazy or his mom checking in. But for some stupid, lame, annoying reason I will it to ring. Just this once, wanting her to think of me the way Pris did with the Cherry Pepsi.

It doesn't happen so I decide to stop moping and dial the damn phone. Mom picks up after the fourth ring.

"Hello?"

My first thought is she sounds the same, which is a stupid freaking thought because why would she sound different? It's not like I've been away for years or something. "Hey, Mom. It's me, Jaden."

And the winner of the most idiotic sayings in a row goes to Jaden Sinclair. Of course me is Jaden. Who else would it be?

"Jaden. Hi. How are you?"

"I'm cool." I cross my legs. "Just thought, you know,

88

you might want me to check in or something. Thought maybe you'd wonder how far we got or want to make sure we're all safe. We are, if you're interested." Heat simmers inside me. Why did I even call her? I should have known all it would do is make me mad.

When she speaks, she has the nerve to sound offended. "Of course I'm interested. You're my son."

But I'm not Mike's.

Why the hell do I even care? I mean, it's not like I really do, but at least then I knew. Now? I don't know anything.

"We're in Salt Lake." I change the subject.

"Good. That's good. Have you talked to your uncle?" Her voice is soft.

"Yeah. I'm supposed to call him when I figure out when I'm flying in. Depends on when we get to New York. He'll pick me up at the airport and stuff."

Heat rolls through my body and I don't want to tell her anything. Don't want her to know who's picking me up or what I'm doing because in my head, she doesn't deserve to know. Not after everything.

But then, hiding inside me, there's a guy who somehow found a damn flame-retardant suit that is soft and feels the need to tell her.

"Good . . . That's good. You'll be happy there."

Will I? I don't know. I could have been happy in

New York. And maybe I can be happy in Texas. Or maybe I'm fooling myself into thinking I'll be completely happy anywhere.

I shake my head. Jesus, I hate all these thoughts. I feel like such whiner. "Okay. I guess, I better go."

"Okay. Bye. Thanks for calling," Mom's voice bounces back at me.

I open my mouth to say, bye, but instead something else comes out. "Are you . . . Are you okay?" Not that she wouldn't be. Actually, things are probably better for her now. I'm sure all Mike ever wanted was me gone anyway.

Mom sounds perky when she says, "Of course, I am. Why wouldn't I be?"

Exactly. Why wouldn't she be?

I hang up the phone and my mind goes back to the stupid piece of paper in my pocket, wondering what the person who lives at the address is like. Wondering, just maybe, if things were different, if they'd be the type who would call me.

CHAPTER EIGHT

We get up the next day and get ready for our rafting trip. I'm totally looking forward to it, and not, at the same time. It's going to be fun, yeah, I know, but there's another little fact that keeps jumping around in my head.

Priscilla in a bikini.

She wore one last summer and I about died. I mean, sexy, right? I'm totally pumped to see one again because . . . yeah, guys are visual creatures, remember? But this is going to be hard on me, too, seeing what I can't have. Hard isn't even the right word. Brutal. Killer. I'm totally going to want to touch. Which I can't and it sucks, so yeah, mixed feeling on the whole raft trip.

We head up to the raft rental building. We're going for one all of us can ride. The trip is only like an hour and a half. Bastian is bouncing around on his feet like he's about to jump in the ring with Mike Tyson during his ear-biting era, and I can't help but let it rub off on me. Adrenaline starts pumping through me as I think about being out there on the water.

"Think you can handle it out there, Doc?" I give him a playful push. "I mean, it's not like I can't pick up the slack for you or anything, but . . ."

"Please, dude. The day you have to pick up my slack is the day hell freezes over. Ninja, remember?"

I laugh because he's such an idiot with that ninja stuff. I open my mouth to say something, but Priscilla beats me to it, sneaking up behind him and sticking her foot out to hook in his. Bastian stumbles, as she says, "Yeah, look at that stealth."

Now I'm laughing even harder. "Pris just went ninja on your ass," I say as he tries to save face by pretending he did it on purpose.

"Whatever. I knew she was there."

She surprises us both by sticking her foot out and doing it again. "Damn it!" he yells, half a smile on his face.

I almost fall, I'm laughing so hard. Aspen, too, but she's actually trying to cover it up.

"Aww, are you alright, big guy?" Priscilla teases, trying to wrap her arms around him.

He starts mumbling something about her kissing it and making it better and I don't know where it comes from, but I hold up my hand for her to give me a high-five and say, "That's my girl."

Priscilla stumbles a little and I actually feel embarrassed. What the hell? I've hit on so many girls. Met so many girls at parties and thrown out so many lines, but it's different saying things to the girl who means something to you. When it's real, you're out there, all vulnerable and shit wondering what she thinks about it or if you sounded like an idiot.

Priscilla doesn't leave me hanging though. She lifts her hand and smacks mine the way Bastian and I would, but my heart is actually thumping. I can't remember my heart ever thumping like that with a girl unless we were touching a whole lot more than this, and I'm sure it went wild then for a completely different reason.

Before it becomes obvious I'm pretty close to some kind of nervous breakdown or something, I grab her, putting my arm around her and pulling her close, like I would have done last year. No one needs to know I'm practically spouting poetry in my brain. "She's the shit. I'm keeping her in my corner." I play it off, but feel like I'm standing in front of a classroom naked or something because both Bastian and Aspen are looking at me with huge smiles on their faces.

I don't even have to look to know Priscilla's smiling too.

What is it they say? If you can't beat 'em, join 'em. I let myself crack one, too, as we go rent our raft.

At the risk of sounding like a Hallmark card, it's really pretty out here. We're halfway through our trip and even though Aspen is wearing a shirt over her bikini, Priscilla isn't. I think she's doing it to drive me crazy. I can't stop looking at the curve of her hips, her legs, and all the smooth brown skin.

It's crazy how many places there are on a girl to explore. Does she know how incredible she looks? All normal and happy, talking with Aspen or talking crap to me and Bastian. It's like she doesn't realize how big a deal she is. What something as simple as licking her lips or hitting my leg can do to a guy. I wonder if girls know that, the kind of affect they can have. Or maybe it's just Pris who has that much power. I don't know.

Priscilla leans forward, the pink strands of her bikini top sliding down her back. I want to touch it. To tickle her with it. Do something to see if I can make her feel even a tenth of what I'm feeling right now.

She and Aspen start talking about something, as though we're in Normalville and I'm not almost dying over here.

"Dude, you're drooling." Bastian nudges me.

"I am not," I try to wipe my mouth all incognito, just to be sure.

He shakes his head. "I was where you are last year, remember? I know my shit. You want her, Jay. You've always wanted her and you're going nuts right now. Seriously, loony-bin crazy. Been there. You might as well give in now."

My eyes jump to the girls who are still in their own little world and not realizing Bastian's calling me out. We're at a calm part of the water right now, so I lean back a little bit and relax. "I'm not giving in to anything. We're friends. That's all. Texas girls are supposed to be hot."

Bastian doesn't even crack a smile. "How stupid do you think I am? I'm your boy . . . or I'm supposed to be, at least. I told you when I started to like Aspen."

I don't know what he wants me to say because it's not the same thing. It's not like I've suddenly *started* to like her. I've known for a long time. And it's not like we can be together because I can't even sort through stuff in my own head, so how would I ever make things work with someone else? Even when I want to do the right thing it ends up wrong and I'm not pulling her into that.

"I don't know. It's different or whatever." I don't look at him as I talk, but be sure to keep my voice real low. "I just . . . know it wouldn't work. Her parents hate me anyway." I shrug, hating that that's true. Why does everyone seem to hate me?

"No one would be good enough for her. They want everything perfect when it comes to Pris, but, hell, they don't even pay attention to her half the time. Between you and them, she'd pick you every time."

She would? I want to ask, but then I realize how needy that sounds. "She shouldn't have to."

Bastian groans. "Be real with me for a minute, man. We're like, turning over a new leaf or whatever. I think it's part of growing up . . . just be real. Do you like her?"

There isn't a hint of a joke in his voice. No laughter on his face, which for Bastian is like a freaking miracle. And for once, I feel like I need to admit it. To say it, just to hear the words come out. "Yeah . . . yeah, I do."

My eyes find the water, the trees, and rocks around us. Anything, but him . . . or her.

"That's all I needed to hear, man." Sebastian moves over to the other side of the raft. "Watch out, Pris. I want my girl back. Go over and protect Jay from the rapids coming up."

I look at him and the jerk actually winks at me. I know I'm screwed because he obviously has something up his sleeve. But when she moves over to sit by me, I can't make myself care.

We hit a rapid. The water is white as it slams into rocks and flies up over the edge of the raft, spraying us.

Even though it's hot outside, the water is cold.

96

Priscilla screams, and buries her face into my arm as we hit another one, more water flying at us. The front of the raft dips down and flies up again as we bump along. I use the oar to push us off a rock, but try not to move too far away from Priscilla, either. Sebastian has the other oar.

My body is pumped as we soar across the water. I see Bastian wobble and almost fall out and I can't stop myself from laughing at him.

We hit another big one and bump hard.

"Oh my God! My shoe just flew out," Priscilla shouts, her pink flip-flop floating away.

By then the rapids are over and the water is calming again.

"Dude! That was awesome. The best one," Bastian holds out his fist and I bump it.

"No shit." I'm soaking wet. Way wetter than I realized I would be.

We're at the end of the trip now, so Sebastian and I steer the raft over to land. We get out and help the girls out of the water. There's someone who works there who takes it and gives us a slip to turn in once we get back. The shuttle ride takes a lot less time than the trip and after buying a couple drinks, we're walking to the car.

"That was a blast." I tell them as I look over at Pris. She's jumping around as she walks and I realize her feet are probably hot on the pavement. Bastian and Aspen are walking in front of us a little bit, holding hands.

Stopping, I grab her arm. "Jump on."

She looks at me like I'm crazy and I want to tell her yes I'm a glutton for punishment, offering for her to get on my back and wrap her legs around me.

The look is gone just as quickly as it came and she puts her arms around my neck and jumps up. Her legs wrap around my waist and I grab onto her, trying not to think about what her silky skin feels like under my hands.

This is what I love about her. So many girls would have played around, pretending to be embarrassed and that they didn't plan on jumping on my back when they knew they would. Or they would have actually been too embarrassed and we would have stood there arguing about it forever. Not her though. She doesn't let anything trip her out. She just climbs on because she knows her feet are hot and wants a cure for the situation.

Yeah. It feels good to be her solution.

We get to the car all too soon and I let her down. We parked in the shade so it's not too hot for her.

"Let's dry off a bit before we get in," Bastian says.

"Oh my God. You're such a girl," Aspen teases.

"So, I don't want my car getting all wet. What's wrong with that?"

We all laugh and then Bastian opens the back so we can grab our towels. We pull ours out while Pris is still searching.

"What the heck. I can't find mine."

We're all wrapped in towels except for her. It's actually a little chilly in the shade, but the black ground will be too hot for her feet if she moves to the sun.

"Here. You can have mine," I tell her, but she shakes her head.

"Just let me in." She nuzzles between my closed arms until I open them and she steps inside. Automatically my arms wrap around her and my head rests on top of hers. Her body is a little tense, but then she shivers and relaxes, pulled up tight against me.

Logically, I know it's just to keep warm. I mean, she already told me she's over me and that's the way it's supposed to be, but that still doesn't stop me from having to move my lower half away from her. Guy, remember? She's gorgeous and half-dressed and totally rubbing up against me all innocently, so, yeah . . . my body is reacting.

Glancing at Aspen, I see her all smiley like she just won the lotto or something. Bastian gives me another wink, like he thinks he knows something he doesn't. Whatever. I know what this is. She's moved on and in a few more days we'll be thousands of miles away from each other. We're friends and I've touched her a million times. There's nothing different about this one.

I hold her a little tighter and she shivers again, before her arms find their way around me too. All I know is, at this moment, I'm actually happy and things feel normal—no, better than normal, and I want to enjoy it for a little while, so I keep holding on.

CHAPTER NINE

We go back to the house for a little while to get ready for dinner. The girls get ready together because . . . Well, I don't know. They're girls and they do stuff like that. It takes Sebastian and me half as long to get ready as it does them, so we're chilling downstairs while they do whatever it is girls do.

I'm wearing a pair of black shorts, long, and they're belted loose and low like I like them. I have on a blue button-up shirt that has short sleeves and my black Adidas. My hair is still wet from the shower and it's getting so long, it hangs in my eyes now.

"What are they doing up there?" I ask as I fall back onto the couch.

"Who knows, man? I try to stay as far away from them as I can when they get like this."

For once I think he might know what he's talking about. I'm seriously tired and I just want to go to dinner and come back and chill.

When I hear noise on the stairs, I open my eyes, not even realizing they fell closed. *Holy shit.* My body lurches into a sitting position and I'm suddenly not tired anymore. She's seriously trying to kill me here.

My eyes start at the sandals on her feet and travel upward to the skirt she's wearing. Up further to her purple shirt. It hangs off her shoulder and a strap from her tank top shows. She's dressed like that before. She's always been more girlie than Aspen, but this outfit? I think it's going to be imprinted into my brain.

"'Bout time," Sebastian mumbles before getting off the couch like he's somehow not seeing the same thing I am. I follow because I don't want to be the only one losing it here. I always notice her, always see her, but I swear she wore this for me. Or maybe it's wishful thinking because she already admitted to being over me.

"Yeah. We're starving here," I throw in so it's not obvious I might swallow my tongue.

We go outside and jump into the Explorer. Priscilla reads off the address and Sebastian puts it into the GPS. A few seconds later we're driving down the road and I'm hoping my body doesn't start to react to Priscilla's legs and how one of them is right up against mine. Nothing says lame like a surprise woody over something you shouldn't get *that* excited about.

The drive isn't too long and I manage to keep myself in check. A few minutes later, we're piling out of the car. There's a bit of a line, but we knew there would be so we chill in line for about twenty minutes before they let us in.

I collapse in a chair when I notice Sebastian pulling one out for Aspen. Yeah they're together and Priscilla and I aren't, but I suddenly feel like an ass for not thinking of it.

"Such a gentleman." She gives me the eye. I'm about to come up with some excuse to defend myself, but then she says, "But then if that makes you like Bastian . . . I'm not sure."

"Hey! What do you mean? I'm the shit." Bastian replies and everyone at the table rolls their eyes because, half the time, that's all you can do when it comes to him. Granted, I'm usually involved, but whatever.

"Please, you have nothing on me." I dust off my shoulder even though that's old as hell. "One of these days you'll catch up, man. Don't worry too much."

Sebastian doesn't have time to answer because the waitress comes up to ask if we want anything to drink. The place is packed and loud just like Priscilla told us it would be.

I order my Cherry Pepsi, Priscilla gets water. I don't get how she can drink so much of it. I mean, it's water. It's not like it tastes good, but it's always what she picks.

After a few minutes she comes back to take our

order. Priscilla and I are on one side of the table and Sebastian and Aspen on the other. Bastian orders, then Aspen, and when they get to our side I tell Pris to order first. It's such a little thing. Half the reason I did it was just to show Sebastian up, but the smile she offers me gives the gesture a whole new meaning.

It's stupid but I wonder if Bastian feels like this when Aspen smiles at him. If it makes other guys feel almost . . . I don't know . . . high when they make a girl happy. Does it make them feel invincible? Like they can take on the freaking world or something? Make their blood run hot and their body tense everywhere?

"Show off," Sebastian sneezes and says at the same time. I hold up one hand to shield the other while I flip him off.

"Maybe you should take some lessons," Aspen tells him.

Sebastian's eyes get all wide. "What? I got your chair. That's way sweeter."

By the way the waitress is looking at us, I can tell she's getting annoyed. Whatever, though. This is our epic trip and I'm going to take every laugh where I can get it.

We're walking back into the house when Aspen looks over her shoulder and says, "Hey, Jaden. The portable

DVD player isn't working. You want to look at it for us?"

I shrug because it's no biggie. I like taking things apart and putting them back together again. Any kind of electronics. "Sure. I can't promise anything, but I'll check it out."

Priscilla's hip bumps mine and I really wonder if she's trying to kill me. "Whatever. You'll fix it. You always do."

Okay, okay. I have the bizarre urge to thump my chest and tell her *damn right*. I'm the man and I can do anything. Really, I'm just in awe she has that kind of faith in me. Which makes me feel like a loser. I mean, it's a cheap, little DVD player probably anyone could fix . . . or no one. I don't know yet, but I like that she thinks I can do it.

But the guy in me wins. Not sure if it's because he really won or because he's easier to let out. "Well, yeah. I mean, I know I'm good, but—"

This time she punches me. "You have such a big head."

"So I've been told," I tell her, biting back my laugh. When she swings at me again, this time I'm ready. I grab her wrist, and damn is her skin soft. How do girls have such soft skin?

We're sort of wrestling around, her trying to pull her hand free and me holding on when I forget there's a step behind us. I trip, going down fast and taking her along. Priscilla falls on top of me as I hit the hardwood floor. I half try to catch her, one of my hands ending up on her waist and somehow under her shirt a little bit.

Talk about soft. Holy crap. I groan because, yeah, she feels good.

"Serves you right if I'm too heavy."

She tries to pull away again, but I don't let her. I use the excuse we're wrestling and I want to win and I feel like an idiot for falling, but really, it's the way she's laying across me. The vanilla scent and the smooth skin.

"Let me go!" she says, but seriously, she's not fighting me that hard. Or maybe I just want that to be true.

Get it together, Sinclair, I keep telling myself.

"Why? I thought you were tough? You tried to be a few minutes ago." It's hard to keep the laugh out of my voice. If there's one thing she doesn't like it's for someone to get the best of her. She's strong like that.

"I can kick your ass!" She's really trying, now. I'm laughing my butt off as we roll around on the floor. It's way too hard, but I don't care. She's pulling away from me and I'm holding her tight and I don't know or care where Sebastian and Aspen are.

Somehow we scoot over so my ass is on the step and when I fall down it, she does too, and her knee comes down hard in my crotch.

"Oh shit!" I let go of her now. My hands are needed somewhere else. It hurts and that's the last place I want any serious damage done.

I'm on my side, away from her.

"Holy crap! I'm sorry!" She rolls me over so I'm facing her. She looks down where my hands are cupping myself before her eyes shoot back to mine. "Umm . . . are you . . .?"

"Injured for life? I think so." Yeah, I might be playing it up slightly. Of course it hurt, but it's also nice to have her worry about me, too. "You may have just killed my chances at making little Jadens."

My eyes find hers, ready to lay it on thick again to score some sympathy points, but that caring look is off her face. Priscilla shakes her head, Spanish flying out of her mouth a million miles an hour. Despite the pain, I laugh a little because I should have known I couldn't pull one over on her. No one can.

"Don't make me laugh. It hurts!"

This time she pushes me before standing up.

"Ouch! Seriously. I'm telling the truth. You maimed me." I'm half-smiling, half-grimacing.

"Good!" She crosses her arms in that sassy way that is so hot, a little smile curving her lips.

"That's cold, Pris. Seriously."

"Wow . . . and here I thought you were this big, strong man. Does poor little Jaden need help up?" She's using her fake-sweet voice.

Okay, time to re-plan. I definitely don't want to come off as soft. "I am a *big* strong man. That's why it hurts so bad." I wink at her. Sure, I'm lying on the floor which probably kills the effect, but whatever.

Priscilla opens her mouth, closes it again, and then huffs before she stomps away.

"Wait," I call, scrambling to my feet. Sebastian and Aspen are nowhere in sight. They must have gone upstairs to their room and I don't want Pris to go lock herself in hers too. "I'm kidding. Well . . . not about the big part but—" I let my words get cut off by the sharp dagger of her eyes.

"I'm just sayin'," I add.

She totally looks like she's trying not to laugh, but she'd never give in like that. She won't let me see that she thinks I'm funny.

"I'm thinking you owe me a favor. I mean, I'm seriously injured here. That at least means I deserve a movie." The words jump out of my mouth before I have time to think about them. I'm glad. Right now, I don't want to think. I just want to react.

By the way she's biting her bottom lip, her eyes all wide, I can tell she's surprised. Guilt tries to push its way in again. She shouldn't be shocked I want to watch a movie with her.

"Umm, sure. Yeah. That'd be cool." Priscilla wrings her hands together like she's nervous. It's so weird—this change with us. I don't want it to be there.

I want to kiss it away, which is all kinds of dumb.

"Cool," I tell her, not able to think of anything else to say. I'm apparently really good with words right now.

"I'm going to change."

She turns and runs up the stairs, like she's going to be late for something. A little confused, I head to the kitchen and grab us each a drink, before I fall onto the couch in the living room and put my feet on the coffee table.

A few minutes later, she comes back down. She's wearing a pair of short shorts and another little tank top thing and man is it hard not to stare at her. "I got you a drink." I nod at the table so I have an excuse to look somewhere else.

"*Gracias.*"

Suddenly, I'm not in the mood for a movie as much anymore. "Want to play a game or something first? I'm kind of feeling like kicking your butt at something."

She picks up one of the couch pillows and smacks me in the head with it. "You're worse than Bastian sometimes. I'm pretty sure I'd beat you, and weren't you trying to be a gentleman earlier?"

I shake off the Sebastian comment. "I am a gentleman. They're honest, right?"

This earns me an eye-roll. "I think we have cards here. That's probably all."

I groan. Yeah, I want to play something, but cards don't sound that exciting. "Eh. I guess."

Then, Priscilla jumps up, as though my words electrocuted her. "I have an idea." Her bare feet carry her to the kitchen and I follow behind. Priscilla grabs a stool and reaches high in one of the cabinets. I've seen this kind of scene in a movie before. Usually it's some woman cooking dinner and she reaches real high and the guy about dies from lust. I used to shake my head and laugh, but right now, I could totally die from the desires shooting through me.

Her shirt pulls up a little, giving me a glimpse of what it's covering. It's all dark brown and cinnamon and I'm totally craving something spicy.

Unlike those movie girls, Priscilla steps down with a bottle of vodka.

"What are we playing?"

She gets down from the stool before she answers. "Go Fish."

"What?" She's already heading into the living room again and I'm right there with her. "Sort of ironic, don't you think?"

"That we're playing a kids' game with alcohol? Absolutely."

She sits on the floor at the coffee table and I fall in next to her. She's so freaking down to earth. That's what I love about her. The girl could have anything she wants, but she's sitting on the floor with a bottle of vodka, no cups, and about to play Go Fish with a guy with a pierced face who just got a cast removed that he got from punching people.

I wish I could tell her.

"Should we grab Sebastian and Aspen?" I ask her.

"No. I'm sure they're enjoying whatever they're doing much more than this."

Yeah. She's probably totally right on that one.

"What are the rules here, you card shark?" Last time we played, she kicked all our butts at poker. I'm hoping I have better luck at Go Fish.

"You ask for a card and if the other person doesn't have it, you draw a card and take a drink." She smiles before she starts to shuffle the deck.

"I think I'm liking this game." I rub my hands together. "We might not like it when we're in a car all day tomorrow, but for now, it's bomb."

Once she has the cards dealt I tell her to go first. See? I can be a gentleman.

"Do you have any sixes?" she asks.

I pull my cards down so they're not blocking my face, wink at her and say, "Go fish."

We've played four games and I'm definitely feeling my buzz. Priscilla is smiling into her cards like they're her best friends or something, which tells me she's definitely feeling it too.

"Do you have any kings?" she asks.

"Hell yeah. I am a king." We both crack up laughing. There's a small part of my brain that knows I just said the stupidest thing in the world, but that's the thing about drinking, it sometimes makes the dumb things the funniest.

Priscilla drops her head backward so it's lying on the couch, and she lets out a huge belly laugh. She's holding her stomach she's laughing so hard and I suddenly wish for all the stupidest jokes in the world.

When our laughter finally dies down, she holds out her hand for the bottle and I pass it to her. Our hands touch. Hers are cold but somehow they feel awesome. There's this little cold zap that passes between us. Or maybe it's just me, but then she jerks the bottle back and I'm totally thinking she felt it too.

Priscilla puts the bottle to her lips and takes a huge drink. I hold out my hand and ask for it back and do the same.

"You didn't have to go fish," she mumbles.

Does it make me a loser that I just wanted my mouth where hers was? "Nope."

She looks at me for a minute, her eyes suddenly clear despite the buzz. We just sit there, a table between us that feels like it's an ocean, but nothing at all at the same time.

"You're wearing the eyebrow ring I got you . . . You've been wearing it for a while." Her words come out of nowhere.

I reach up and touch the piercing. "It's badass," I say. Someone else probably would have said it better, but I can't say it any way except my own.

Priscilla tosses the cards to the table. "I'm done." She climbs up on the couch, pulling her legs close to herself.

Since it's easier, I actually crawl over and then pull myself next to her. She shakes her head when I try to hand her the bottle so I set it back down on the table.

Without looking at me, she says, "I'm tired."

I am too, but I don't want to go upstairs. "You can go to bed, if you want."

"I'm good."

"Lay down here then." I try to stand up, but she puts a hand on my shoulder to stop me. Even if I wanted to, which I don't, there is no way I could move right now. Her touch has frozen me. Possessed me. And there's no way I'll be the one to break the contact.

I settle back into the couch and then without looking at me, she lies on her side and puts her head in my lap. It feels like forever since she's looked at me, even though it's only been a few minutes. She's facing the TV and I'm looking down at her. At the way her hair falls and the way her lips turn and the way her chest rises and falls as she rests.

My hands are freaking begging me to touch her. To kiss her or to do *anything* but I still can't make myself move.

"Will your parents notice the vodka's gone?" It's the only thing I can think to say. My head tilts back so I'm looking at the ceiling. I can't keep looking at her or I'll do something really stupid.

She's quiet for a few minutes and I wonder if she fell asleep. Finally I hear, "No. They won't notice."

"Good. If they do, blame me. Tell them you didn't know I took it or something." The last thing I want is for her to get into trouble.

"They won't notice, Jay. They don't notice much of anything."

There's a sadness in her voice that I don't understand. A sadness that makes me open my mouth and say, "My dad fucking hates my guts. Well . . . I guess he's not even really my dad." It might be the wrong thing to say, but she gave me a piece of her, so I want to give her a little bit of me too.

I feel her head turn on my lap and know she's looking at me. Know she wants me to talk, but I can't, so I let myself be the loser I am and just shake my head without letting myself turn away from the ceiling.

There's more of a pause . . . I can almost feel the seconds tick by as I wonder if she's going to ask. As I wonder what made me even say what I did.

"He's an idiot," she finally says. "Anyone would have to be stupid to hate you." And then she rolls over again, almost like she's trying to burrow into me. Like she wants to be a part of me and I totally want that, too.

I don't even try to open my mouth because I know I can't say anything. My throat is closed, so instead I put my hand on the side of her head. Automatically, my fingers tangle in her hair.

"I'm glad you came, Jaden."

"I'm glad I came, too."

And then my world goes black.

CHAPTER TEN

S omething pokes my cheek.

"Goldilocks, wake up," someone says in my ear.

Sebastian's voice is not what I wanted to wake up to today. My eyes struggle to open. I know it's early. We planned to head out at a decent time, but the sandpaper behind my lids also has to do with the bottle of vodka sitting on the coffee table.

"Open your eyes before I pour water on you."

That makes my eyes jerk open. I wouldn't put it past him to do it. Amazingly, I manage not to move because I don't want to wake Priscilla. Her head is still in my lap, but she's facing my stomach now, her arms tucked up underneath her and against me. I feel bad she slept on the couch all night. I should have woken up and brought her up stairs.

"Psst. Are you paying attention to me, Romeo?" Sebastian is whispering, I assume, so he doesn't wake her.

"Romeo?" I rasp. Ugh. My mouth is totally dry.

Why did we think it was a good idea to play Vodka Go Fish?

His eyes shoot toward Priscilla and then back at me. He's got that cocky look on his face that says he's not only jumping to conclusions, but he's up to something, too.

I shake my head. "It's not what you think, Cupid." If he's going to play the name game with me, I definitely have some stored away for him. "Where's your bow and arrow?"

"I'm about to shoot your ass with it."

Just then, Priscilla starts to stir on my lap. "Be quiet before you wake her up. She's not going to be feeling too hot today and needs to get some more sleep." My fingers itch to push the hair off her face, but I hold myself in check.

"Aww, aren't you sweet. Bet you weren't thinking about Woodstock and me like that when you guys drained that bottle." He stands up straight and crosses his arms.

I don't bother to reply to that. "What time is it?"

"Five."

Which means we're supposed to leave in an hour. I know we need to clean this place up before we go. My head pounds at the thought of doing anything today: cleaning, sitting in a car, or even standing up.

Slowly, I put my hand under her head and scoot out from under her. Once I'm able to stand up, I softly set her head on the couch. Sebastian follows me into the kitchen. "Where's your girl?"

"Upstairs getting ready. I would ask you where yours is, but I already know."

"Ha ha." I run a hand through my hair. "I'm going to clean up a little and then I'll wake her up in like half an hour. That way she only has to jump in the shower real quick before we go."

Sebastian's looking at me with a big ole shit-eating grin on his face.

"Welcome to the club, man. Welcome to the club." He holds out his fist for me and I bump it, trying to figure out what he's talking about.

The twelve-hour drive is not cool. Sebastian and Aspen play the music a little louder than normal and I'm pretty sure it's because they know my and Priscilla's heads are killing us.

I wondered if things would be awkward with us, but she's acting normal, and if she can do it, I know I definitely needed to man-up and just go with the flow. It's what I decided about this trip. All those thoughts crowding my brain, I want to shove in a back corner, lock them away, be like the rest of them. Like Priscilla, Sebastian and

Aspen. The way they've always thought I was until recently.

Kind of hard to hide getting picked up at the jail and a busted-up hand.

Around seven we pull up at a hotel in Grand Island, Nebraska. Tomorrow we should only have around ten hours to go and we'll be in Chicago. I can't freaking wait.

Sebastian kills the engine and turns to face Priscilla and me. "We're gonna get our own room. Cool?"

I look over at Priscilla and when she shrugs, I tell him it's all right. A few minutes later, we're in our room while the others are next door. It's one of those rooms with a connecting door and our room has two beds. If this had been a movie, they would have been full so we would have had to share a bed. Why doesn't stuff like that happen in real life?

Priscilla goes into the bathroom to take a bath, so I start screwing around with the DVD player. It's easy for me to get it apart and mess around with all the bits and pieces inside. It's close to an hour later, when she finally comes out smelling all clean with wrinkly fingers. I have the urge to kiss them, which is really strange. I've never wanted to kiss a girl's fingers in my life.

"Feel better?" I ask.

She comes to stand behind the chair I'm sitting in. "Yeah. How about you?"

I nod my head while I move around some of the little pieces to find what I'm looking for.

"You tore the whole thing apart, Jay."

"I know." I look up at her and wink. "Trust me. I can get it back together again."

"I know you can."

Her words do something funny to my chest. Make it sort of tight or something, which makes me feel like an idiot so I ignore it.

"Do you want to take a shower?"

Unable to hold it back, I grin at her. "Are you offering?"

She rolls her eyes, but I swear there's a smile hiding in them. "Perv."

Now I'm the one smiling because there's definitely some kind of happy in her voice. I know it doesn't mean anything because even if she wasn't over me, I'm not sticking around, but I can't help reveling in the way it feels. I want to hold onto the good because it usually only happens with the three people on this trip with me.

"You like it. Don't pretend you don't." I dodge her fist and jump out of the chair.

"You're such a boy. *Stupido*." She adds and I'm laughing.

Just to keep giving her shit, I wink at her, before I grab my bag and head into the bathroom. I take a quick shower, brush my teeth, and then I'm back in the room a few minutes later. I'm really wanting to take my shirt off because it's sort of hot and I don't usually sleep in one, but I'm not sure if I should.

"I'm going to call my parents to check in. Did you call your mom?" She doesn't look me in the eyes as she speaks which is a total dent to my pride. Does she feel sorry for me? Is she thinking about what I said to her last night? That's exactly what I want to avoid, why I don't want to talk about the fact my whole life the man that lived with me called me a piece of shit and my mom didn't do anything about it.

"I'm cool. I'm gonna go grab us a drink and some ice." This time, it's me avoiding eye contact with her as I head over to the connecting door and bang on it.

Sebastian jerks the door open. "What the hell, Jay. You're killing the mood over here. I was trying to romance my girl."

"Don't listen to him, Jaden!" Aspen calls to me. "I'm reading and he was passed out!"

"Whatever." Bastian scratches his head. "Was just getting a little rest before the action started."

I laugh at him. "Come on, *Romeo*," I toss his word back from earlier. "Come get a soda and some ice with me."

"Aww, the next thing we know they'll be going to the bathroom together, too!" Priscilla yells.

Aspen starts cracking up. "You guys are such good girlfriends!"

"Thanks, man. You just turned us into girls." Despite his words, Sebastian is pulling a shirt over his head and then following me.

"Ma wants you to call her," Sebastian says as we start down the hall. "She said she tried your cell, but it's turned off."

I forgot I'd done that. I pull it out of my pocket. There's a missed call from Courtney, but no one else. "I will."

"She said to tell you to keep that shit on. She wants to be able to be in touch with you."

"Did she call it shit?"

"Ha ha."

We get to the soda machine and I buy myself a Cherry Pepsi and water for Priscilla. "You want anything?"

"I got it."

I don't know why, but his words bug me. "I can buy you guys a soda, asshole."

"Dude, I totally just missed something. I never said you couldn't, but I also think I'm pretty capable of putting a dollar in the machine, too."

So I might have overreacted. Whatever.

"I really wish you'd quit being all 'I am island' and talk to one of us about whatever the hell you've got going on, Jay. Seriously." Sebastian leans against the wall, opens his soda, and takes a drink.

His words not only shock me, but I'm sort of grateful for them at the same time. I'm not sure which emotion to focus on. "Love has turned you into a sap. Since when do you want to talk about what's in your heart or whatever?"

"Since I started to grow up. You should consider it sometime. Makes things a whole lot easier, Jay."

The last person I need a lecture on growing up from is Sebastian. "Are we living on the same planet? You never take anything seriously."

He takes another drink before replying. "I take Aspen seriously. My mom. Pris. And your dumb ass. Seriously, man. We've had fun the past few days. Are you really going to bail? It's supposed to be the four of us. Don't pretend you're not having a good time with Pris."

"You're the one who says I need to grow up. Maybe this is how I'm doing it. You're not supposed to be with your best friends forever. That's not the way the real world works, Sebastian. Life might be easy for you, but it's not for the rest of us." *But I want it to be. I want to stay with you guys. I want to be someone.*

"You're nothing but a waste of space. A loser. One of these days everyone is going to wake up and see that, you piece of shit."

Is it so wrong to want to walk away before they do

it? Before Priscilla's parents decide they don't want me around their daughter for more than just a stupid graduation party?

Sebastian shakes his head. "You're right, man. I couldn't possibly know what it's like to have a hard time. There's no way I could actually be there for you or some shit. You might as well keep it all locked in. It's better that way."

My body is tense. Anger sweeps through me.

But it's also twined with the stupid feeling to open my mouth and talk to him. To tell him I don't feel right. Don't feel as good as them and that I can't shut up Mike's voice in my head. That I can't stop wondering if my real dad threw me away too.

That I don't want them to do the same.

"Shit," Sebastian pushes his hair out of his eyes, "I feel like a freaking girl here. We're fighting like crazy. It's just . . ." He shrugs. "Never mind. Come on. Let's go back to the rooms. I want my girl and I'm pretty sure she's missing me. I'm sure you want to get back to Pris, too." Sebastian winks.

I shake my head. Of course he had to get that last jab in. I don't bother to set him straight, but I also can't stop wondering what he was going to say.

I'm still pissed when I open the door to our room. It all gets forgotten when I see Priscilla standing with her back to me and hear her arguing on the phone.

"It's my choice. You promised. It's too late now."

It might be a janky thing to do, but I stand in the doorway, listening. It's not like I'm eavesdropping. She can turn around and see me at any second, and it's not like I snuck in.

For a few seconds she holds the phone, listening to whoever is on the other end. "Don't worry. I get it. I know it's not what Daddy wanted. You don't have to keep reminding me."

This time her voice has an added sadness that I don't like. It makes me open my mouth and say, "You okay, Priscilla?"

She whips around to face me, but she doesn't speak, obviously listening on the phone again.

"It's Jaden," she says, giving me a small smile. I close the door behind me and that's when it starts. Her voice is raised and she's speaking in Spanish, which means she doesn't want me to know what she's saying.

I've never heard her talk so fast. Her free hand is flying through the air, which means she's really mad. When she tries to smile at me I know whatever is going on, has to do with me. How stupid am I? I never should have opened my mouth and said something without knowing who she was speaking to.

She locks herself in the bathroom for a few minutes, making me wonder what's going on. Are they giving her a hard time for hanging with me? Telling her I'm all the things Mike told me I am? There's no way I'll let her get in trouble for me. I'll leave before I let that happen.

When she finally emerges, I'm sitting on the edge of my bed, leg bouncing up and down like I'm on something. My heart is doing the same thing, banging around because I don't like to see her upset.

Priscilla is pacing the room back and forth like I've never seen her do. She's controlled and steady. She's supposed to have it together and it kills me to see her unsure. I want to make it better.

"*Dios*! That makes me so mad!" she says, still with the back and forth.

"You wanna talk about it?" Those words feel weird coming out of my mouth because I never want to talk about anything, but I don't want her to be like me. I don't want all that shit trapped inside her until she wants to explode.

As though my same train of thought is driving through her head, she looks at me with this funny expression on her face. Her eyes are bigger and browner than I've ever seen them. It's hard to read her face. Anger, maybe? Confusion? And then pain.

That's when it happens. Like a trick of the eye, someone snaps their fingers and tears start pouring down her face. I don't think, don't even pause before I push to my feet, walk to her, and pull her in my arms.

Priscilla's face buries into my shirt as she lets go; big, sobbing cries that vibrate through me. Wetness seeps through my shirt, but I don't care. All I want to do right now is make it better. Take care of her. That's what you do, right? When someone is important to you, you take care of them. You try to take their pain away, pull it into yourself if you can, because it's easier to fight her demons for her than to risk someone scarring her.

I would take them all on if I could.

Nothing else matters right now so I shush her and rub her back and let my hands go through her hair. I'd do anything to make her feel better. Cut myself open and let her see all the secrets inside me. Whatever it takes. Whatever she needs.

But she keeps crying and I wonder if I'm doing something wrong. Not saying the right things. When her legs weaken and she goes slack against me, I stand for her, holding her against me as I back us up to the bed.

I lay down with her and pull her to me like I have a right to her or something. Like she's mine when we both know she isn't and never will be.

My lips actually fucking tingle, wanting to touch her forehead, her hairline, down until I find her lips. Which totally isn't what she needs right now, and makes me feel like a dick for thinking it.

"Why won't I ever be good enough for them?" she asks into my shirt.

I try to pull away so I can look at her, but she doesn't let me. Her hand is knotted in the back of my shirt and it feels incredible to have her hold me this tight.

"There's no one you're not good enough for, Priscilla."

This just makes her cry harder and I wonder how I screwed that up.

"Shit . . . I'm sorry. I just mean . . . You have to be wrong, ya know? They'd do anything for you. You're good at everything. There's no way you're not good enough for them. Maybe it was me? Because I'm here?"

This makes her pull away enough to look at me. "I don't care what they think about you. And they may be willing to give me anything, but that's not the same as *doing* anything for me, Jaden. It always comes with strings. Do you know the only reason I got to come to New York is because I agreed to one year of what I want to do, and then I have to go pre-law?" Some of that fierceness is coming back into her voice, but it's all wrapped up in the pain.

"You don't want to be a lawyer." She doesn't. I used to think she did because of her dad and because she's so good at arguing, but it's not her.

"That doesn't matter. That's what's expected. Everything is always for show and not because they give a shit. My graduation party? That wasn't for me. It was for them. To look good. I was there for twenty minutes and no one noticed when I left. All I wanted was to be with you guys and they tried to take that away from me because of—"

Because of me. Her unspoken words hang in the air. Because I'm the one who isn't good enough.

"Me. It's okay. You can say it." I'm still touching her hair and her back because now that I've started, I'm not sure I can stop. "I'm used to it, Priscilla. If my own parents don't give a shit about me, how can I expect yours to?" I immediately want the words back and not even because I regret telling her. Somehow, I'm glad I said it, but this is about her and I don't want to bring my stuff into it.

Our breaths mingle together. I feel the heat from her body as she's tucked against me from head to toe. Her hand squeezes tighter and even though it bites into the skin of my back, I want to feel it more.

"I told you, I don't care what they think about you. They don't know you."

I want to tell her I care. Not for me, but for her. I don't want to be a strike against her. I don't want to hold her back, but I can feel her and smell her and it's all too much. I need more. Just like last summer, she pulls me, guides me, steers me like my beacon and I can't stop myself dropping my mouth to hers.

CHAPTER ELEVEN

I come down too hard and too fast and our teeth clank together. I feel like an idiot. I've kissed a ton of girls and never done that, and I immediately want to pull away, but she doesn't let me. Priscilla's hand slides through my hair and her lips move against mine and all I can think is *more*.

More of everything.

I search my brain for a switch to turn off my thoughts. I don't want to think about anything but her right now as I slide my tongue into her mouth. I taste mint like she brushed her teeth and salt from her tears and still I think, *more, more, more*.

Her hand tugs at my hair and she makes this tiny little noise in her throat I don't hear, but feel. Feel her lying next to me, kissing me as we lay on our sides in the bed.

I kiss her deeper, letting my tongue get intimate with every part of her mouth. And she does the same, tasting me and then letting me taste her.

All I can think is, this is kissing. *This*. Which is stupid because, like I said, I've kissed girls, lots of girls, but none of them came close to what this feels like.

Instinct takes over and I roll us, Priscilla on her back and I'm on top of her. She flinches a little when I settle in and I'm sure it's because she realizes what I have going on under the belt.

I pull back, even though it's the last thing I want, but then she whispers, "No," and leans up to find my lips again.

This time, it's me who wants to burrow myself inside her. I kiss her lips, behind her ears, her throat. I lick her skin and touch her hair and she's doing it all to me too.

My hand ghosts between us and touches the softness of her stomach. I explore and feel all those dips and valleys and curves that are Priscilla. And then when I know I'm going to explode if I don't stop, I leave an inch between our lips when I say, "I'm sorry. I shouldn't have—"

"I'm not," she cuts me off.

"Okay, I'm really not, either." And I'm not and we both laugh and this time when I roll, I pull her so she's half laying on me. One leg is flung over me and one arm is over my chest. She's in the crook of my arm and I touch her hair, thinking how much I like it straight, but realizing I like it just as much when it's curly.

After who knows how long passes, she says, "I just want them to love me for me . . . I just want to be good enough."

"You are good enough, Priscilla. If they can't see that, it's their fault." But what I really want to tell her is that I'd love her for her. Hell, maybe I already do. I can't though. I can't give them another reason to treat her like she doesn't measure up. Not when I *know* I don't.

I think she starts to cry again, so I just hold her tight. Tight enough so she knows I'll always be there. Hoping she can feel how much I care by the way my arms wrap around her. I think about the paper . . . the address and I think maybe, just maybe, I can tell her about that, too.

We sleep all night with the light on. I thought about getting up to turn it off, but I didn't want to leave her and it didn't seem to bother her so I stayed. She fell asleep before me and it took me forever to do the same, but finally I did.

Much too soon, I hear a bang on the door and know it's Sebastian and Aspen to wake us up. I pull my phone out of my pocket and try to text him one handed to chill the hell out and that we're awake, but Priscilla starts to stir and I know there's no need.

"Shut up, Bastian!" she yells before easing away from me.

Thanks, man.

Her hair is all messy and she stretches, her shirt pulling up a little bit and I worry about showing her just how much I like the view, so I sit up.

"Hey," I say, which is completely stupid.

"Hey."

"How are you feeling?" I raise my hand to touch her hair, but stop myself. It's all kinds of dumb and I need to remember that.

"Better. I don't know why I freaked out last night. You'd think I'd be used to it by now."

"You shouldn't have to get used to it."

I stand up, feeling like a loser and not sure what to do or what to say. Like always, Priscilla saves me, standing and putting her arms around me. I pull her into a hug, like we did with the towel in Utah, my chin resting on top of her head.

"Thank you . . . for last night and all."

"Any time, Priscilla. You know that."

She looks up at me funny. "I like it when you call me Priscilla."

I like it, too. Sometimes I wish I could say the things I think in my head. Or that she could read my mind because it would make things so much easier. "Okay." I pull away from her. "We should probably get ready before Sebastian has an aneurism."

"Only if you do me a favor."

"Absolutely."

She hugs me again, her cheek resting on my chest. "We only have a few more days, yeah? I know that. Just don't think too much, okay? Let's just . . . *be*. Whatever happens, happens, ya know? I'm a big girl."

I feel like such a pussy that she ever has to say something like that to me. What is wrong with me? She's right though. I'm not going to freak out. I'm not going to think about anything. The switch is still off, so for now I'm fine. Bending forward, I let my lips cover hers. Our tongues tangle for a minute before I make myself pull away. "Come on, Priscilla. Let's get ready."

"I'm totally going to moon him." Sebastian turns in his seat.

I groan at the same time as Aspen says, "Bastian! Don't."

"Yeah, Sebastian. Don't, unless you want me to go blind and wreck your car."

Priscilla laughs from the passenger seat. We've been having a contest on who can get truckers to honk or people in other cars to laugh. Yeah, it makes us sound like we're five, but who cares? It's fun and it's a long, boring drive through the rest of Nebraska and Iowa.

"I'm winning here and you guys don't think I'm not going to bring out the big guns to seal the deal?" Sebastian says, still moving in the backseat.

"True. I'm sure your ass looks funny as hell," Pris adds. "I'm sure it would make me laugh my butt off."

"Hell yeah. That's my girl," I say and then I realize what just came out of my mouth. I totally just called her my girl in front of everyone. Yeah, we made out last night. Kissed a little this morning, but we've been normal ever since. All I need is for Sebastian to get some stupid idea in his head and start blabbing his mouth like he does.

The whole car is quiet for a few seconds. I use driving as an excuse not to look in the back at Bastian and Aspen, but I can't stop my eyes from darting over to Priscilla. She shrugs like it's nothing and gives me a small smile before she says, "Didn't we make a no-nudity rule at the beginning of this? If not, we should have. I don't want to see Sebastian's white butt."

"Hey! I have a nice ass! Don't I, baby?" Sebastian whines. Aspen rolls her eyes.

"Dude, you're the only guy I know who would say that."

"That's because I don't care what people think."

"Word," I say because he doesn't, and I don't either.

Do I? I'm not sure. I never thought I was the type to give a shit, but I'm doubting that right now. I don't know what it is about him saying that right now that struck me, but it did.

I totally care what people think. That pisses me off.

"Why do you look all tense over there?" Priscilla pats my leg.

How does she do that? It's crazy how she can read me. I wonder if that's a girl thing or a *her* thing. "I'm cool." Really, I'm not. I'm suddenly in the mood to prove I don't give a shit what other people think about me.

A little while later, we stop for gas. Sebastian fills the Explorer while the girls head to the bathroom. After I buy Priscilla and me some candy and soda, I head around to the side of the building. It's stupid that I decide to call her right now, but for some reason, I need to.

I set the bag on the ground and call home. Three rings later I know I've made a mistake.

"If it isn't the bastard. What do you want from us now?" Mikes voice seethes through the phone.

I almost hang up. It's obvious he wants to talk shit to me or he wouldn't have answered the phone, but . . . I don't know. I want to try to prove him wrong. Show him I don't need them. That I never did.

And I also just want to talk to my mom. I hate that side of me—that I can still need her when I've never been a priority in her life. Three parents, and I couldn't score one who gives a shit. What does that say?

"You? I don't need shit from you. I want to talk to my mom."

He's quiet for a second and I wonder if he's surprised. If he actually thought I would be crawling back to them. I'm sure he missed his verbal punching bag, but then he opens his mouth and says, "I guess it's too bad she doesn't want to talk to you. You might think it's just me, you little shit, but it's not. Did you ever think she was counting down the days until she could get rid of you? That she regretted everything about you? It's not like you ever gave her anything to be proud of. What have you done, boy? What have you ever done that matters besides making our lives hell?"

My drink drops out of my hand, but I manage to hold on to Priscilla's soda. I don't know why those words hit me so hard—why they happen to scream above all the other insults imprinted into my brain. Was she really anxious for me to go? Did I ruin her life?

Do I really not matter?

"Mike! I'm ready!" I hear Mom in the background.

Ask him who he's talking to. Ask if it's me. Say you want to talk to me.

"Finally getting it, aren't you, boy?" Mike says, and then he hangs up.

My hand begs me to squeeze, to crush the phone.

I don't matter. I don't matter. I don't matter.

God, I feel like such a pussy. I can't breathe. My chest feels tight and the emotion makes me angrier. The urge to yell crawls up my throat. I want to hit something—the wall, the ground, anything. I want some other kind of pain so I don't feel the one inside.

I fall back against the wall, his words still slamming into me.

"Jay? You over here?" Priscilla walks around the corner and my lips automatically stretch into a smile. Not a real one.

"Hey, I was just—"

"What's wrong?" she cuts me off, stepping toward me. Her hair is tied up in a ponytail and I remember what it felt like to have my mouth on the skin of her neck.

"Nothing. I'm cool. I got you something." I hold up her drink like an idiot.

Priscilla shakes her head, mumbling Spanish. Seriously. Girls who speak Spanish? Hot.

I look around to make sure I don't see Bastian or Aspen. I just need to be normal. Act normal so we can drop this and get going, but I'm not sure what to do. I want to reach for her, pull her to me, because

139

that's okay, right? After last night, I should be able to hold her. Or just hug her? I've hugged her a million times before. Instead I shuffle my feet, not sure what to do. "Hey, you usually only speak Spanish when I piss you off. What did I do this time?" I wink, trying to show her I'm being playful and I need her to do the same, but she doesn't laugh. Doesn't smile.

She just looks . . . sad.

"Hey, what's wrong?" I don't hesitate this time when I pull her to me. She wraps her arms around my waist and I rest my chin on top of her head. "Did you talk to your parents? Did they do something?"

"I don't want to sound like a wuss," she says against my chest and I can't help, but think about how good she feels there. There's something about having a girl lean on you—trust you—that makes you feel invincible.

"Pfft. Yeah right. Like you could ever sound like a wuss. You're fierce." And she is. Totally fierce. Even how she is with her parents. It's awesome.

We stand there for a few seconds, not talking and just . . . being? I don't know, but she doesn't pull away so I'll hold her as long as I can. Soon I'll be too far away from her to even *see* her.

Finally, after she lets out a long sigh, she breaks the silence. "I just want you to trust me, Jay. That's all. I wish . . . even if it's not me . . . you'd let someone in."

She tries to walk way, but I reach for her hand and pull her back. "Hey. I trust you." I do. I think. No, I know I do, but I also know they don't need to hear all my shit, either.

Her eyes narrow and I know she's about to give it to me. She'll gripe and I'll sweet talk my way out of it and we'll be good.

But she doesn't. She looks sad again. "It doesn't have to be me," she adds again.

Huh? Who else would it be? There isn't anyone else. "I said I trust you. There's nothing wrong." I'm starting to get annoyed now. Why does everyone always bug me to talk? What's it going to do? It's not going to change Mike or anyone else.

She shrugs. "Okay."

"What do you mean, 'okay'? Aren't you supposed to give me crap?"

Priscilla draws her hand free and crosses her arms.

"Hey." I try to pull her to me again even though I know I shouldn't. I know she's not my girl and never will be. "I thought we weren't fighting. I liked last night a lot more." I give her half a grin, but she doesn't return it like she's supposed to.

She uncrosses her arm and pushes her hands in her pockets. "We're not fighting, Jay. And I liked last night, too."

She doesn't say anything else to me. Priscilla turns around walks back to the Explorer.

We might not be fighting, but for some reason this feels worse. What is it with girls?

Sebastian is driving the last couple hours before we get to Chicago. Aspen's up front with him, leaving Priscilla and me in the back.

"Here's your drink?" I hand her the water I got her. She takes it from me and smiles. It's a normal smile, but something feels wrong about it. Something feels wrong about that thought, too. What's wrong with me? Something is wrong with her smile?

Sebastian puts in a CD and we rap and sing along. He makes dumb jokes and I tell him they're dumb and he does the same thing to me.

They laugh and give us shit and it's all normal in a way. Like always, they're my buffer—they quiet Mike's voice in my head and make me feel okay, but somehow it's still not right. I can't stop thinking about how she looked at me and the slump of her shoulders, and the way she keeps looking at me, but turning away when I return her stare.

Like she said, we're not fighting. We're okay, but not at the same time.

When we get to the hotel, Sebastian and Aspen disappear into their own room, and Priscilla and I get two beds again, but all I can think about is sharing with her. Talking to her or kissing her until things aren't off anymore.

It's nuts how I never kissed her until last night. I mean, obviously I thought about it. She's a gorgeous girl and I'm a guy and she's *Priscilla*, but now that I've done it, I can't stop thinking about it. I keep thinking of ways I can make it so we have to do it again.

Pris lounges on the bed in her pajamas, watching TV, and I work on the DVD player. I have the thing practically put all the way back together, I've been so in the zone. We've talked a little and she asked me to get her ice so I have no reason to be freaking out like I am right now.

I take another forty-five minutes and the DVD player is together again. "Wanna see if it works?" I ask.

"Sure."

Priscilla scoots over and I sit down on the edge of the bed before leaning over to plug it in. She's next to me, so close we're touching. Her legs are tucked beneath her and she belongs there, curled up beside me, like we're a couple like Sebastian and Aspen, and I would be free to touch her whenever I wanted.

And I want to.

Touch her, I mean.

I'm praying the dumb thing will work. It's stupid, because honestly, who gives a shit? It's not like it's important or will mean I'm suddenly worthy of anything, but I want to be able to do *something*.

"Is it gonna work?" I ask just because I need to talk.

"Absolutely. Stop fishing for compliments. Here." She pushes my hand out of the way with hers. "I'll do it."

Before she hits the button, I laugh.

"What?"

"We're acting like this is a huge deal or something. Like it really matters."

Priscilla looks at me—inside me, something. "It is a big deal. Plus, aren't you supposed to be all cocky or something? *I'm the man. I can fix anything* and then start grunting or whatever?"

I push my hair out of the way so it doesn't block her from my view. "Well, no shit. We all know I'm the man, but no grunting. I'm not down with that."

She smiles and it's a real one. A Priscilla one. "Stop stalling and let me push play."

I hold up my hands and she takes advantage, pushing play. A couple seconds later, the thing comes to life.

"It works!" she says.

"It might not keep working."

She nudges me. "It works now and that's something, Jay."

I have never wanted to kiss her as badly as I do right now. My lips burn. My body aches. But I don't know if I should do anything or not. What am I supposed to do?

"I'm tired. We're getting up early tomorrow. We should go to bed," she says.

We're going to be in Chicago for a few days, but she's right. The girls want to be up early every day for whatever their girl reasons are.

"Okay." I get up, turn the DVD player off, and put it away. Priscilla climbs into bed and once she's there, the blanket all pulled up to her face, I turn the light off. Before climbing into my own bed, I pull off my shirt.

I swear it's thirty seconds later I hear her get out of her bed and then my bed dips.

"Scoot over." Priscilla pushes her way into my bed. I have to admit, it's not like she has to push hard. Before I know it, she's under the blanket, her head on my bare chest.

She feels incredible.

And I'm totally confused as to why she just climbed into bed with me. "You were mad at me earlier," I finally say.

145

When she sighs, I feel her breath brush against my chest. "I wasn't mad at you, Jay. I was . . . I just wish you'd let me in. I just want you to let me in."

Her words bring an ache to my chest. It hurts and I feel like a piece of crap. *Why can't I let her in?*

"So you're not mad?" I manage to say, hating the weakness in my voice.

"I'm not mad. I'm . . ."

And she doesn't even have to say it because I know. She's *disappointed*, and as far as I'm concerned, disappointment is much worse.

CHAPTER TWELVE

"Why is it every friggin' time we go somewhere, you guys drag us shopping?" Sebastian pouts as we walk to where our trolley will pick us up. Funny, last time we went shopping at the beach, he'd been so busy trying to suck up to her that he didn't complain once.

"Because we're girls and we like to shop and you guys love us so you'll deal with it," Aspen replies to him.

"Absolutely. And you love me so you'll deal with my complaining, too," he adds and then they start making moon eyes or whatever at each other. It's like a cartoon with little heart bubbles floating over their head.

It's ridiculous.

"Save that stuff for somewhere else, okay? I already feel a little woozy," Priscilla says.

"Word," I add, because I want her to know we're on the same page. Which is probably as bad as Sebastian and Aspen, but at least it's in my head.

"You're just jealous 'cause we're the shit," Bastian tosses out and I know it's meant to be a joke, but

I'm sort of jealous. Which just makes me feel like a jerk.

"Whatever."

We got these trolley passes so we can get off and on at any stop, to explore whatever we want. The first stop is, of course, shopping because we pretty much let the girls get away with anything.

We get to the stop right as the red trolley pulls up. Sebastian and Aspen jump on and I step out of the way so Priscilla can get on first. I mean, I woke up with her all curled up against me so I figure I should at least be a gentleman. Though I was one last night, too, as much as I wish I hadn't been.

When we climb on, Priscilla and I sit in seats in front of them.

"This is so cool!" Aspen says. "I think I like Chicago better than New York."

"No way. New York is incredible. Remember when we went to check out apartments . . ."

I block out Priscilla talking to her. Aspen's parents and Courtney and Phil brought Sebastian and Aspen out a few months ago to get things sorted out. Priscilla's parents let her go with Aspen, of course, even though they had realtors who do that stuff for them. And probably did. I never took the time to ask. Sebastian and Courtney tried to get me to go with them since it would be my place too, but I hadn't wanted to blow the money. It's not like my parents would have helped. It's also not as if I would have let Phil and Courtney spot my ticket like they'd wanted to.

So yeah, I'm the only one who hasn't been to New York. I was the only one who didn't make that trip with them. I'm so tired of being *that guy*.

"So what? We just jump off this thing when we're ready, or what?" Sebastian's comment pulls me back into the conversation.

"What the hell are you talking about, man?" I turn to look at him.

"It's the Hop On, Hop Off tour. So we just jump off, or what?"

I look at Priscilla. We both look at Aspen, then all six eyes at Sebastian before we crack up laughing. My stomach starts to hurt I'm laughing so hard. I really wish I could stop so I can tell him what an idiot he is, but it just keeps going.

"What's so funny?" Sebastian looks back and forth between us.

It makes us laugh harder and then another thought pops into my head. These are my favorite times. Yeah, I know guys aren't supposed to think like that or maybe we're not supposed to say it. Or hell, maybe it's neither and it's just that we don't but none of that matters. What does matter is I'm never as happy as I am with them. I never feel like I can be me—even though I'm not sure I like who that person is, but, yeah, it's going to suck to not be by them. To not laugh at Sebastian or have Aspen do something nice for me or have Priscilla to keep me in line when I need it.

This is my crew. My people. And I hate that I have to leave them.

I hate that I don't think I can make myself stay.

"Do you really think people just jump off a moving trolley whenever they want? I mean, what if they're kids, or old people?" I finally manage to get out between laughs. "I mean, I'm not saying people haven't done it, but you seriously thought that's what it meant?"

"What the hell else is a hop on, hop off ticket?"

Aspen touches his leg. "You're so cute when you're being ridiculous," she says, which makes him pout and the rest of us laugh harder.

Finally when we're able to calm down, Priscilla explains to him that it means we can hop on at any stop or hop off at any stop.

Me? I just sit back and enjoy being happy.

We go to Magnificent Mile first, which really is Michigan Avenue. Boulevard. Something like that. The girls definitely think it's magnificent. I'm pretty sure I couldn't afford a hotdog here. We go to clothes stores and shoe stores and even freaking furniture stores as we walk down the eight-block money pit.

Sebastian and I hang in the back most of the time, letting them do their thing. We give each other shit and pretend to try on clothes and even get kicked out of one of the stores.

Other times, we sit back and watch them. It's probably not something guys talk about too often, but sometimes we just like to sit back and watch girls. They're so different to us, all soft and smooth and . . . I don't know, girlie. Yeah, I know it sounds stupid, but seeing her makes me remember what it's like to touch her. I totally want to do it again.

When lunch time comes around the girls want Italian. We find a little place to eat that's out of the way. I offer to buy Priscilla's lunch for her and she lets me without hesitation. I wonder if she knows I need that, or if it's a coincidence. I have a feeling it's the first one. It's crazy how she can realize things I would never be able to tell her.

After lunch we find another trolley stop and ride down to one of the old neighborhoods with all the really cool architecture.

"Wait, wait. Look at this one." I make them stop for the millionth time.

Sebastian elbows me. "I don't get it. It looks like all the rest of them to me."

"Yeah, I guess. It's still cool though." I'm definitely not an expert on the subject, but it's always been interesting how things are put together. I can't stop myself from wondering what lingers behind the walls, how it was planned and built.

"It's gorgeous." Priscilla looks up at the towering building sort of in awe. I don't know if it's for me or if she's really interested, but I'm actually thankful for it and jealous at the same time. I want her to look at me in awe, which is probably one of the dumbest things I've ever thought.

"It's badass. I like how the covers meet together." I get close to her and point as though she doesn't know what I'm talking about.

She steps closer to me too. So close I can feel her heat as we gaze up.

"You guys aren't going to start making out, are you?" Sebastian cuts in. "Ouch!" He stumbles backward when Aspen hits him.

"Bastian!"

"What? I'm just sayin'." He winks at me.

I don't know what he thinks he's winking at. We obviously weren't going to kiss and if we were, he totally ruined the mood.

He stands there like he's thinking for a second and

I actually cringe when he opens his mouth again. You never know what's going to come out of Sebastian's big-ass mouth.

"Actually, that's a good idea. You know you guys want to. Kiss, fall in love, come to New York with us. Happily Ever After. The end."

"*Stupido*," Priscilla calls him.

"Has anyone ever told you that you have a huge mouth?" Aspen adds.

"It's a joke. He won't kiss her. I think he's lost his touch."

He just smiles all wide like he's proud of himself and I have the urge to sock him. Okay, maybe that's partially an excuse to touch her again, but I turn to pull Priscilla to me, shocked when she beats me to it. She's grabbing my face and her lips slam into mine. It's almost like our first kiss, all messy and unskilled, but we find our rhythm quickly. We start moving together the way we're supposed to and, like always, she goes straight to my head. All too soon she's pulling away. She looks at Sebastian and flips him off.

I'm thinking we need to teach him another lesson in case he missed it the first time, but instead I wink at him. "Please, man. You don't lose skills as good as mine. I could teach you a lesson or two."

For the first time, Sebastian is speechless. He's looking back and forth between me and Priscilla and finally he yells, "Hell yeah!" And then the dumbass attacks me. He tries to jump on my back, but I dodge him. His arm hooks around my neck and freaking ruffles my hair like we're five and I shove him off. It's then I realize I'm laughing my ass off and he's laughing and the girls are laughing.

It's awesome.

We start down the street again, Sebastian still talking crap and still trying to beat me up. When the girls aren't paying attention I look at him and say, "That doesn't mean I'm staying in New York."

He gives me another huge smile. "Whatever you say, man. Whatever you say."

Our next stop is the Chicago History Museum. Not that I'm a museum kind of guy, but it's another one of those things a guy will do for a girl. Priscilla loves history and I know she really wants to go.

This is probably going to make me sound like an idiot, but I had no idea museums were this big. Or maybe not all of them are, but I swear it's like the size of my hometown. There are different rooms for different kinds of exhibits and of course she wants to go into all of them.

So we do.

I kind of enjoy it, too.

Aspen and Sebastian go off on their own. I'm

assuming it's because Aspen knows she can control him better when it's just the two of them. Or maybe it's because they've been leaving us alone together a lot on this trip. Whatever the reason, they're somewhere and we're here and we're going to meet up with them in a little while.

We're there for a few hours and they have some kind of special going on about magic. Magicians walk the hallways, performing magic tricks. They've stopped Priscilla a couple times and showed off their skills. It's so funny to watch her. It's almost like she's a kid. She gets these smirky little smiles on her face like she's up to no good. Other times it's huge, stretching across her face.

It's cool to watch her—to see her enjoy something so much.

Is this what she wants to do? I wonder. I can't believe I never thought to ask her. We have all always known she didn't want to be a lawyer, but I've never asked her what she *does* want to do.

We look around some more and finally end up meeting Sebastian and Aspen in one of the rooms where they're doing a magic show. It's all about history and Chicago's part it in. I never would have thought I'd like something like that, but it's fun.

Sebastian and Aspen stand next to us. She's in front of him, leaning back with her head on his chest. Sebastian's arms are around her, holding her close. I look at Priscilla standing between us. I'm not holding her hand. Not doing any of the things Sebastian is doing with Aspen. She looks at them too and I wonder why I can't be man enough to do what he's doing. Wonder why we can't stand the way they stand and be happy the way they're happy.

It just reminds me again I'm not the guy she deserves.

CHAPTER THIRTEEN

Sebastian threatens to try and jump off the trolley as we head to the hotel. I threaten to push him. Neither of those things happen. "It's hot. We should go swimming or something," Priscilla says when we're in the hallway of the hotel.

"Sounds good to me." I open the door to our room. Once everyone is changed, we meet down by the pool.

The girls mostly lay in the chairs while Sebastian and I swim, which is pretty confusing since I thought we came down here because of the heat. They get in about thirty minutes before we're done.

"Let's play chicken!" Sebastian gets a huge smile on his face.

Priscilla on my shoulders while I get to hold her thighs? I'm totally in.

Her feistiness takes over and we win, two games to one.

I'm pretty sure Sebastian threw the last one just to have an excuse to dunk Aspen. Not that she seemed to mind. Personally, I was good with the whole riding-on-my-shoulders thing.

We get out of the pool and head around the building to go back to the room. Aspen is walking closest to the wall and when we walk around a corner, she says "Ouch!" and drops everything in her hand. When she bends over, red trickles down a cut on her leg.

The stuff is out of Sebastian's hand in a second and he's kneeling on the ground next to her. "What happened, baby?"

"Something cut me. Whatever that is sticking out the side of the building."

"Let me see it." He's kneeling on the hard ground on his knees, but he doesn't seem to care about anything except her. He eases her hand away and there's a gash in her leg. Bastian grabs the closest thing to him—his shirt—and starts to clean her up.

"Is it bad?" her voice sounds wobbly.

"Don't look at it, okay? We're good."

Aspen doesn't do well with blood and we all know it. Priscilla and I stand there watching them. Aspen looks up so she doesn't see the blood. As Sebastian alternates between looking at her to make sure she's not watching and wrapping her leg in his shirt.

It's crazy to watch them together. I've never really seen anything like it—the way he takes care of her. The way she takes care of him, too.

"Come here." He stands and lifts Aspen into his

arms, hers going around his neck. "I think you might need stitches, Woodstock."

"I'll go grab the keys."

"I'll go with you, Jay, and I'll get some clothes for us." Priscilla and I run up to the rooms. We get the keys to the Explorer and I grab some clothes for Sebastian and me, while she does the same for her and Aspen. We're back out at the SUV a few minutes later. I drive with Priscilla in the passenger seat and Sebastian holding Aspen in the back.

It's the emergency room which means the place is crazy busy. Priscilla and I get dressed in the bathroom, but Sebastian doesn't want to leave Aspen. She does have a shirt over her swimsuit now, though.

He keeps whispering to her and stroking her and all I can do is wonder what that feels like.

An hour and a half later, we're still in the waiting room. Both Sebastian and I have gone up to see how much longer it will be, but no one has an answer for us.

Finally they call her back, but the fact is, we still don't know how long we'll be waiting.

"Why don't you guys go? I'll text when we're done. You can go grab something to eat." Bastian then gives his attention back to Aspen as he carries her through the sliding door.

"What do you want to do?" I ask Priscilla as we

climb into the car. The sun is setting. She must be hungry by now. We haven't eaten since lunch. "Are you hungry? We can grab something to eat."

"I'm okay. Maybe we can go walk around for a little while?" She turns the radio down.

The neighborhoods around here are kind of weird. Each of them has their own name, but it doesn't take us long to find a busy area that looks decent. After I park, we get out and start to blend in with the crowd.

A few minutes later she says, "Sucks about Aspen. It's kind of crazy seeing Sebastian with her, isn't it? I mean, it's been almost a year, but it still surprises me sometimes."

Her hand accidentally brushes mine as we walk. Or, at least I think it's an accident. It's so strange, overthinking stuff like this. "I know. I was thinking the same thing. It's cool, but different."

We're quiet for a few more minutes and I can't stop myself from trying to figure out what she's thinking. Is she wishing I could man-up like Sebastian? Is she done thinking of me like that and whatever has gone down on this trip is just for fun? Whatever it is, I can tell it's serious by the way she bites her lip. She does that when she's thinking.

"So . . . have you talked to your mom since we left?" Her voice sounds unsure.

How lame is it that she has to be nervous to ask me if I've talked to my mom? "A little."

"How's she doing?"

"Okay." Happy. Better off. Not worried about me.

"Is she planning a trip to Texas any time soon?"

I'm trying to figure out how we got on the subject of my family. And why we're still on it. The last thing I want to spend my time with her doing is talking about home. But I also know it shouldn't be this way. This is Priscilla, one of my best friends in the world and the only girl who has ever really meant something to me. I should be able to open my mouth and talk to her.

Priscilla starts in again, "I have, in case you were wondering. I talked to my mom again today. I told her I might change my mind . . . that I can't promise them I'll be a lawyer."

My feet plant to the ground. "Wow. That's huge, Priscilla." I'm not surprised though. Not when it comes to her. She always stands up for herself. "What did she say?"

We start to walk away. It's late enough that the crowd is thinning out. There's some kind of music coming from up ahead of us.

"That I'm being ridiculous. That it's what I've always wanted. What she means is it's what Dad wants. They never ask what I want. It's assumed and then shoved down my throat." Her head is held high but her voice shakes slightly. What's it like for her? Does she feel any of the same things I do?

"I'm sorry."

"It's okay." She shrugs.

"No." Stopping, I grab her hand. "It's not. You can do anything. Don't let anyone tell you differently." Annnd, I sound like an idiot. "I mean it."

"I know you do." This time it's her who stops walking. She's still doing the lip-biting thing that drives me wild. Her hair is messy and she's in a t-shirt and old shorts, but I don't see anything of that. I just see her.

"You can too, Jaden. You know that, right?"

How did I know this conversation would go here? She goes from looking sexy to feeling sorry for me and I hate that look. She's the last person I want looking at me like that.

With my best smile and a wink, I say, "Damn straight I can."

Her head isn't high anymore and I hate it. Why can't I just be real with her? "I'm sorry. I wish . . ." But I can't say anything else. There are people all around us and I'm obviously emotionally stunted.

The music is louder; there's a jazz band playing in this little square. People are gathered all around, some of them dancing and stuff. I lean toward her because I can't keep myself away. My forehead touches hers and she jumps slightly as if she's surprised. "Dance with me?" I ask her.

She nods against my head. We lock hands and walk inside the little gate. I pull her close, close as I can get her and her hands lock behind my neck. "It's hard . . ."

Even though she doesn't reply, she holds me tighter and I know she gets it. She knows what I'm trying to say. I also know it's not good enough.

Priscilla comes out of the bathroom after brushing her teeth. Her hair looks like she did something to it. Not styled it or whatever, but it doesn't look as frayed as it did after swimming. We've been quiet most of the night. Aspen has ten stiches in her leg and Sebastian's been spastic about taking care of her.

"You ready for bed?" I ask.

Priscilla nods. She climbs into one of the beds. I hit the light to turn it off and then stand there like an idiot. Which bed do I get into? I don't want to assume anything. We've slept together the past couple nights, but that was because she was crying and then because she climbed in with me. Now, it's my choice.

And I know where I want to be.

"Can I sleep with you?" Damn, I sound like an idiot. I should have just crawled in. Or gotten into my own bed. Why did I ask like that?

"Yeah."

I let out a breath I didn't know I was holding.

Pushing the blankets aside, I climb in. She curls up against my side like it's her home—where she belongs. My arm goes around her and her head fits in that little crook perfect. She smells like Priscilla. Like the girl I've always known.

I don't know what I'm supposed to do here. If I should just hold her or kiss her. We're in this weird place and I'm not sure either of us know where it is. But I know I'm going to hate leaving it.

"What do you want to do?" I whisper into her hair, then I let my fingers run through it.

"Umm, what do you mean?"

"In life. I've never asked. I don't know why I didn't ask. I know you don't want to be a lawyer, but what *do* you want to do?" For a second I wonder if the question is stupid, but when you're friends like us, things like that shouldn't be dumb.

"I want to be happy," she says. Her voice cracks slightly when she says it and I squeeze her tighter. "My parents . . . they're not close to each other. They go on vacations and buy the right things and buy me the right things and expect the right things out of me, but I don't know if they're happy, happy. Like with each other—or me. I don't want to be about those things. I want to be with the people who matter and I want to worry about the things that are really important and not what other people think I should."

Her words are like knives, stabbing into me, poking and prodding and taunting me. I want that, too, but I don't know how to get it. Maybe that's where the taunting comes in. I'm not strong enough to get it. To do what I need to—if I even know what that is. It's hard to imagine myself that way.

But they're also freaking awesome too. The things she wants. They're incredible just like she is.

"*Dios* . . . That sounds stupid, right?" She tries to sit up a little, but when my hand starts to comb through her hair again, she relaxes.

"No."

"You meant a job, though. I'm not really sure. I like history. I like working with people. I just want to feel like I have time to figure it out. Logically I know I do, but there's so much pressure at home."

Her answer surprises me. I thought she knew everything. That she had it all figured out.

"What about you, Jay? What do you want?" Her hand tightens as she clutches my side. It's almost like she's afraid I'm going to disappear.

I am . . .

"I'm not sure either. I'll probably end up working with my uncle or something."

The conversation ends after that. I keep stroking

and she keeps squeezing. Soon her breathing evens out and I'm sure she's close to sleep. "Priscilla?" My voice comes out almost raspy.

"Yeah?" I hear sleepiness in her voice.

"I just want to be happy too."

We're spending the whole day at the Navy Pier. Sebastian and I are pumped. The river, rides, food. There's not a whole lot better than that. The place is crazy busy and huge. I didn't expect it to be so big. There's stuff everywhere, people everywhere and I know there's no way we're going to be able to do it all in one day. We decide to try and do as much as we can.

The girls decide they want to see the circus. I'm not going to lie. I'm not real stoked about the idea, but once they get started, it's pretty cool. It's the Cirque Shanghai and they can do some pretty wild stuff on a motorcycle. Priscilla sits really close to me and once when she gets excited and leans forward, she puts her hand on my thigh.

"Umpf," I mutter when Sebastian elbows me in the ribs. I look over at him and he's got that cocky I-told-you-so look on his face, his eyes darting back and forth between Priscilla's hand and me.

He's such a friggin' idiot.

Shaking my head, I ignore him.

After the circus is over and we've gone outside, Priscilla grabs my hand and drags me over to a building. It looks like some kind of theater or something and there's a courtyard, too.

"Oh my God! They're playing Beauty and the Beast! That's my favorite!" Aspen is attached to Sebastian. Not because she wants to be, either. I know her leg is bothering her.

I groan. "You guys picked the circus. Please don't tell me you're going to drag us to see Beauty and the Beast, too! We're moving to New York. We can go to the theater there!" It's not until everyone looks at me all funny that I realize what I said. Slip of the tongue, I tell myself. That's all.

I try and shake it off by looking at Sebastian for him to back me up. At first he's looking back at me, his head all high like he hears what I'm saying and he agrees. He crosses his arms and I wait for him to say something like 'hell no' to the whole Beauty and the Beast thing, but then Aspen tugs on his arm.

"Come on, Bastian. It's my favorite and I can't be on my leg all day anyway."

"I can't believe you played the leg card." I nudge her gently. I definitely don't want to see this play, but I don't want her to be in pain either. Sebastian will be all crazy and protective if that happens.

Bastian shrugs. "I'm in. Just don't tell anyone we know. I have a reputation to uphold."

Aspen does her swoony-Bastian thing and Priscilla laughs and I just sit back and watch it all.

We grab tickets before heading into the courtyard to see a Disney movie. Okay, a play, but still.

It's not going to start for a little while and since we're outside, we decide to grab something to eat as we watch. The girls sit down and Sebastian and I head out for food.

"Change your mind yet?" Sebastian asks when it's just the two of us.

"Change my mind about what?"

"New York. Pris. Bailing on us. Take your choice."

I turn to him. If it was anyone else, I'd be pissed, but this is how we are with each other. "Dude, you remind me of those old ladies in the salon who gossip all the time. What's with all the talking lately?"

"What do you mean? You don't talk. I'm just trying to do anything to keep my boy with us."

It's then I realize I'm sort of abandoning him. In a lot of ways it doesn't matter, but we've been tight forever. We've hit on girls together and got suspended together and snuck out together. We got drunk for the first time together. Almost got killed by a girl's dad at the same time. We were supposed to do New York together, too.

I groan and push my hair out of my face. "It's not that easy, man. And it's not like I'll never come out and kick it. I just . . ." Don't know how to be around Priscilla and not want her? Feel like an outsider with the people I shouldn't? Can't keep tagging along? I'm obviously a pussy.

"You're screwin' with my record, man. The only other hook-up that ever meant anything is my only failure and you're blowin' it."

It takes me a little to catch on. I shove him. "Dumbass." It suddenly makes sense to me why they've been leaving Priscilla and me alone so much together. Sebastian is still trying to play around. "It's not a game, man."

He shakes his head. "You think I don't know that? I'm not an idiot. Which is also why I'm doing what I'm doing."

There's never any arguing with him so I leave it alone. Then another thought jumps into my head. My heart starts to slam and I don't know if it's a good kind or not. "Priscilla doesn't know, does she? I mean, she's not in on it or whatever." Would she kiss me to try to get me to stay? No . . . not her. She's not like that.

Sebastian laughs. "You do know her, right?" He shakes his head and then adds, "You call her Priscilla all the time now. You didn't used to. What's up with that?"

This time it's me who shakes my head. I'm not

going to get into this with him right now. Or ever. He won't get it. Will he?

"It's her name? I don't know. You never wanted to talk so much before you got with Aspen. You're getting soft on me." Hopefully this will lighten things up. I give him hell and then he'll give me hell and then we'll forget that he wants to talk about stuff I don't want to. Easy as that.

"Maybe I should have, ya know? Maybe things would have ended up a whole lot different if none of us would have let you keep all that shit inside for so long. Maybe things would have been the way they're supposed to."

I stop walking, but Sebastian keeps going. He doesn't get too far when I try to catch up to him, wondering when it was he got so far ahead of me. And proud of him for it, too.

CHAPTER FOURTEEN

I don't understand girls. I might have talked crap to Sebastian like I do, but I really don't. We're sitting here watching the play and Priscilla is crying. Not a cry, cry, but her eyes are glassy and once in a while a little drop will spring free and slide down her dark skin. It's a girl and a beast and I totally don't get it. I'm sure there's something else going on here, but whatever it is, it's beyond me.

Still don't like to see her cry though.

I sit back in my seat and put my arm across the back of her chair. She's leaned back so it's easy for my fingertips to brush her shoulder. Totally love that she always wears tank-tops.

I lean over and whisper, "You're leaking."

A partial smile tilts her lips. "You're a jerk."

I may be a jerk, but she doesn't have tears in her eyes anymore. I don't move my arm.

"I'm ready for rides now. Anyone else?" We step out of the courtyard and start to walk toward the rides.

There aren't tons, but it's still cool and probably better than Beauty and the Beast.

"I'm in," Priscilla pipes in beside me.

"I'm not sure I'm up for it," adds Aspen.

"What? You have to ride something." I'm not ready to go back to the hotel yet.

A guy bumps into Priscilla and she stumbles a little. I pull her to my side. "Watch where you're going, man."

He gives us a dirty look and keeps walking.

Priscilla doesn't detach herself from my side. "Are you sure you don't want to try a ride or two, Aspen?"

Aspen shakes her head. "No. I'm not really feeling well."

Sebastian wraps his arms around her waist and pulls her to him. "I'll go back to the room with you." His mouth is against her neck as he speaks to her.

I eye him, trying to figure out if this is part of his plan. If he's still trying to play Hook-up Doctor with me and Priscilla, but he gives all his attention to Aspen.

"Sorry, guys. We'll see you in a little while, okay? We'll text if I start to feel better." Aspen gives Priscilla and me each a hug before they walk away. The bummer is it makes Priscilla move away from me.

"At least you didn't wuss out on me," I tell her. I can see how happy she is. "What do you want to do first?"

"My choice?" She gives a fake sweet voice.

"Absolutely."

"That's what I thought." Priscilla gives me a wink and then loops her arm through mine as we start to walk. "I want to go miniature golfing."

"What? You're a cheater. I thought we were riding rides."

"It's not like there are a whole lot here."

I shrug. "True."

Quite a walk later we're at the golf course. After paying we start the game. On our first hole I get a par three in four shots. Priscilla gets it in two.

On the second hole it's another par three and she somehow gets a hole in one while it takes me three. She beats me on the third too. "Dude, what are you? An undercover golf pro or what? Are you hustling me, Mendoza?"

"Hustling insinuates I pretended to be bad, which I didn't. If you would have asked, I would have told you I happen to be amazing at mini-golf. You, Jay, just assumed you would win."

"What?" Instinctively I grab her wrist as she's pointing at me. My fingers ring around it. "I didn't assume anything and you haven't won yet. I'm just getting in the swing of things." I pull her to me, "Get it? Get in the swing of things?"

Priscilla rolls her eyes, laughing. "Do you realize how corny that was?"

"I made you laugh, didn't I?" I'm sort of chuckling too and it feels good. Right.

"True." She nudges me with her hip. "I love it when you're like this."

There's a second when I want to ask her what she means, but I get it. I know what she means and I like it, too. "Who wouldn't? I'm pretty damn good company."

She laughs again when a family steps up behind us. "Excuse me? Are you going to play?"

We let them pass. Anyone who catches up to us, we let pass too. We're not in a hurry. I shoot a ball in the water, lose one, and have to steal another. Priscilla laughs so hard at me she trips on a fake rock. The whole time, we laugh.

And when she beats me, it doesn't feel like I lost at all.

From golf we head to this crazy maze thing. Priscilla holds onto me the whole time through twists, turns, mirrors and all sorts of things. It doesn't take long for me to get us out of there. I consider beating on my chest, but figure it might be a little overkill since the thing was probably made for kids.

We have these huge cheese steak sandwiches for dinner that are bomb. I seriously want to eat in Chicago for the rest of my life.

It's getting dark out now—even more people than earlier littering the place as we head back up to Pier Park to ride the Ferris Wheel.

She leans against me as I wait in line and I can't stop myself from holding her. From thinking about the fact that we'll be in New York soon and I'm supposed to leave.

Jesus, what if it hurts her worse now? What if she thinks this means more than it does? No, I don't mean to think of it that way because it means more than anything, but I don't know if it means I can stay.

"Pretty soon they'll get tired of picking up your slack, kid. It won't take them long to realize what I've always known. You're not worth it. You're not worth anything."

"Your real dad didn't want you either." I shake my head. I don't want to think about them getting tired of me—about them walking away. Realizing that I'm not worth it. No. I can't stay.

"Tickets?" The man working the line holds out his hand and I hand him the tickets.

Priscilla and I climb in and she curls up right against me, smiling. Damn this girl is strong, fierce. She's not afraid of anything and I love her for it. The ride starts and I man-up enough to link our hands together. We watch the park as we go higher and higher, lights and water and people.

"It's gorgeous up here." She drops her head to my shoulder.

"For sure." It sounds freaking stupid, but it's like we're invincible up here. No one can touch us and we can do anything, *be* anything. Problems are so far away. Mike's voice only a faint whisper in my head that I am actually strong enough to block out.

Up here, I could be something.

There are buildings in the distance, so much to see. As we circle around and around I take it all in. Look at it all and it doesn't matter that my thoughts are seriously girly right now.

All too soon the ride is over and we're walking through the crowd again.

"Today has been perfect," she tells me without looking my way.

"It has." And then I realize I need to lighten the mood. It has been perfect and I don't want to ruin it like I always seem to do, with too many bad thoughts in my head. "I mean, how could a day with me not be perfect? When you think about it, it's practically impossible."

Priscilla tries to hit me, but I dodge her. "You can't catch me," I tease. We're getting closer to the exit. I'm glad our hotel is within walking distance.

"*Stupido*," she says in that playful voice I love so much.

I stop and she lunges for me, only for me to twist

out of her reach again. "Don't try to best me, Priscilla. I'm perfect."

As I try to get past her, she grabs my shirt. Damn it. She's good. Trying to pull away, I stumble a little. Priscilla trips after me and I fall against one of the buildings.

"Mr. Perfect isn't too good at staying on his feet." She steps closer. My back is to the wall and she's standing right in front of me.

And she's gorgeous. Dark, stormy eyes. Sexy lips.

"I stayed on my feet. If you didn't notice, I caught you."

Shaking her head, she says, "No, the wall caught you. I was never in danger of falling."

I can't stop the grin that spreads across my face. My skin feels hot, tight almost. I feel her eyes like they can somehow scorch my skin. "Whatever you need to tell yourself." Without being able to stop myself, I pull her toward me. She comes easily.

I want to kiss her as bad. Want to feel her lips against mine with the force of the need surging inside me. With everything in me, I slam the door on all the other thoughts that plague me and I do it. My hand slides to the back of her neck and buries deep in her hair.

Then, my lips find hers. She tastes spicy. Feels perfect as our tongues play tag. Her hands squeeze my sides. Her scent surrounds me. There are no people, nothing, except for her.

Pulling back slightly, she kisses the side of my mouth, then the other. I take her lips again in short little close-mouthed kisses when my whole body is jonesing for so much more.

"See? Perfect," my words whisper against her mouth.

Priscilla laughs and shakes her head. My arms are on her shoulders, locked behind her neck. I don't know what makes her do it, but hers slide down my body and then she sticks her hands in my pockets. The paper crumples as she touches it.

A smile tilts her lips and she says, "What's this? Do you have some girl's number in your pocket, Jay? Don't make me hurt someone."

Jesus, it's stupid. I don't even know why, but my whole body freezes. The door in my head swings open and Mike's words come tumbling out. How can I tell her I'm a big enough loser to carry around the address of the dad who didn't want anything to do with me?

"What's wrong?" her voice is concerned now. Usually it makes me feel like someone that she can read me so well. This time, I hate it.

"Nothing," comes out of my mouth while my brain is screaming, stop being so weak! Open your mouth and tell her. You can tell her anything. Didn't I think about telling her days ago? It's so much easier to think about something than it is to actually do it.

When I try to pull away, her grip on my pockets

won't let me. It feels like an eternity before I hear her whisper, "Why?"

Before I get a chance to reply her hands are out of my pockets and she pushes me. "Why!" This time with more anger. "Why won't you ever trust me?"

She gives me three heartbeats to reply. I actually count because I can't speak. I hate the hurt in her voice. The pain in her eyes. And then she turns and walks away.

CHAPTER FIFTEEN

One second later I'm pushing off the wall and right behind her. "Pris—Priscilla! Wait!" I jog after her. I don't get it—why this one thing made her so mad. Or maybe it's everything. Maybe what Mike said is true and she's finally had enough. Finally realized I'm not worth it or it's too much work or—I don't even know. The only thing I do know is I have to catch her. Have to try because this is Priscilla and I can't stand the thought of her hating me.

"Wait!" I call, but I've already caught up.

She whips around and yells, "No!" and then storms away again.

People are looking at us. Clearing the way as we push through the rest of the park. I don't care about any of them. The only thing that matters is fixing this.

We clear the park and we're on the street heading toward the hotel. Her feet move so quickly it's almost hard for me to keep up with her. She's pushing herself, I can tell, so I push myself harder.

The hotel door hits the wall she pushes it open so hard. Everyone in the lobby stops to stare—probably wondering what I did to hurt her. I hate that they're right.

"Why are you like this?" Her voice breaks as I push my way into the elevator with her.

"I'm sorry." The words make me feel weak. They sound weak. All I do is apologize and I never do anything to fix it. Why can't I fix it? "That's why I didn't think it was a good idea for us to mess around. I didn't want to lead you on."

By the way her eyes widen and then start to glisten, I know I've said the worst thing I could say.

"Lead me on? *Lead me on*?" Her hands meet my chest and she shoves hard, making me hit the back of the elevator. "Fuck you, Jaden!"

Ding!

The elevator doors open and she's out. I know I have to catch up or she'll lock me out of the room. Priscilla shakes as she opens the door before trying to close it on me. Maybe a better man would let her, but I know I can't let her lock me out. I need her to understand. Need it more than anything.

"Ugh!" She rips her hands away from the door and walks farther into the room.

I close it behind us, searching my head for the words. Trying not to concentrate on the crazy thump

181

of my heart or the pain spreading through my chest. "I didn't mean that, it's just . . . it wasn't really a girl's number, Priscilla." Why did I say that? It's not what I wanted to say.

"You really think I don't know that, Jaden? I know you better than you seem to know me. That's not the point."

What is? I want to ask her. Tell me what to say or how to fix it and I will.

"You know I didn't think that, either. It's just easier for you to focus on that and I can't . . ." She shakes her head, puts her hands to her forehead. "I can't do it. It's so hard. Why is it so hard?"

She's crying now. Priscilla. The girl who can take anything is crying over me. How many times will I hurt her? How many times will I make her cry? "It's me. Not you." I lean against the table, trying not to look at her. "That's why I didn't—it's not—I knew I would screw it up. I knew I wasn't good enough for you."

How can you fully believe words, but hate to say them so much at the same time? My pride is punching me, wearing me down because I want to be good enough. How can I say those words in front of her? Prove to her everything I've always known? It's easier to pretend I think I'm more than I know I am.

"Huh." She crosses her arms. "I don't think it's

you, Jaden. Obviously it's me. You wouldn't kiss me at the party last summer. We were so close, but you stopped it."

How can she think that? How could I not want her? "What—"

She cuts me off. "It doesn't stop there, though. Something I'm doing isn't enough for you to trust me or feel the same way I do about you."

My body is a cracked mirror, lines spider-webbing out from the central breaking point. My chest, my head and the rest of me does the same. How can she think she's not enough for me?

Priscilla pulls open the sliding glass door and steps onto the balcony. It's a nice room. Way nicer than I could afford without them. My brain is yelling, screaming and cursing at me to tell her. To stop being such a pussy and tell this girl what I feel. What's in my head. Maybe she can block out Mike's voice. Hell, block out my own.

Pushing off the table, I follow her. My hands are sweating and I'm breathing hard, but when I try to speak, my voice hardly comes out. "How can you think that?" *How can you not know you're more than enough? You're everything.*

"How can I not?" She doesn't bother to turn around. She's looking out over the edge of the balcony. A wind slides over her, making her hair blow. "No matter what I do, it's never the right thing. Never the right key to get inside you."

Suddenly, I'm angry. My fists tighten. My heart pounds harder. My head hurts. I'm pissed at Mike. At Mom. At who the hell ever my dad is. I'm pissed at me.

And when my mouth opens, I can't hold it back. I don't know if I want to stop all the words that start to pour out.

"What do you want me to tell you, Priscilla? That my dad is an asshole who hates me? That I've spent my whole life hearing how I'm a piece of shit? That I'll never amount to anything? That I'm not worth anything? That he calls me every name in the book?"

Her body freezes, but I just keep going.

"My mom did nothing to stop it. My fucking *mom*, who is supposed to love me and take care of me, but she loved him more!

"Do you want to hear about how his voice is always in my head? Always making sure I know my friends are better than me and he's better than me. That the whole damn world is better than me! No matter what I do, I can't stop hearing it!"

I feel like I'm going to burst out of my skin. My body is on fire. I'm burning from the inside out, but I just keep going.

"I broke my hand on his face when he told me he

isn't even my dad, did you know that? That some stranger has tortured me my whole life and my mom let him? That my real dad didn't give a shit about me either, but I still carry his fucking address in my pocket everywhere I go? What kind of man does that?"

At this she turns. Her eyes are red, swollen, as tears pour down her face. I want to kiss them away and be angry at her for them at the same time.

"Don't you do that. Don't look at me like you feel sorry for me. Not you, Priscilla. That's exactly what I don't want!"

I try to turn away, but she grabs my arm so tightly her nails dig into my bicep. "He's wrong! I don't care what he says, he's wrong about you, Jaden. How can you not see how incredible you are?"

Her words make me suck in a deep breath because I want them to be true. I want to use them to battle his, to break them down and stab them until only hers remain, but his have a harder punch. Yell louder.

"Do you not see how much Sebastian loves you? He's your best friend. It's killing him to think of you leaving. And Aspen? You stuck up for her when Bastian hurt her. You stood by her. How many guys would do that, Jay? How many would back up their best friend's ex, even if she was right?"

I shake my head. "Anyone would have! He hurt her and I knew he cared about her. That was nothing."

She takes a step toward me, still crying, but I can see her trying to be strong.

"It was something. And Courtney? She loves you like a son. Roger, too."

"Not your parents."

Another step closer.

"That's their problem. Not yours. Jaden, you have such a huge heart. You—"

"They didn't want me," pulls out of my throat again. The words are broken and painful and I hate them, but they're true.

Another step. I feel her and smell her.

"*I* want you. I need you to know that. Those other people—they don't know you. Or they won't see you. *I* see you. To me, you're everything."

Everything? Something? Anything? All those words make me feel incredible. Make me wonder if she could be right. And she sees me? How many times have I thought that about her? "Why? Why me?"

I don't even have to explain my question because she gets it. Gets me. "Because you're you. Because you'd hurt yourself before you'd hurt someone else. Because you're an awesome friend and an incredible son. You fought for me, and took care of me."

"I hurt you."

"You hurt you more."

I manage to lift my hand to cup her cheek and

brush away some of the tears there. There's nothing like it. Like being the one to wipe her tears. That alone makes me feel like something.

Priscilla covers my hand with hers. Heat fuses us together.

"Nothing's the same without you, Jay. Senior year wasn't the same. This trip wouldn't have been the same. New York won't be the same."

It's amazing—the thought that I can make a difference or people can care about me that much. I don't know if I believe it, but I know I want to. I want to more than anything.

I jump when a loud boom explodes and then reds and blues fill the sky. The fireworks from the Navy Pier light out over the water. Ignite the sky, the same way her words ignite inside me.

Priscilla turns around and leans into me, her head resting against my chest. My arms wrap around her, holding her as tight as I can.

And we watch.

I'm still confused. Lost. Mike's voice is still there and Pris's parents are still there and the paper in my pocket still haunts me, but somehow, I don't feel as empty inside. I don't feel quite as alone in it. My words connect us now and give me a strength I didn't know they would. Is it like that for everyone? Trusting in someone and letting them see the monsters inside you? I don't know. All I know is it is with her.

"It kind of feels like they're just for us," she says as more fireworks pop and crack and color the night.

I don't know how I'll feel tomorrow, or in an hour, or five minutes. I don't know if Mike's voice will flare up or if I'll freak out again, but right now, in this second, it feels like more than the fireworks are for us. It feels like everything is.

When they're over she turns in my arms, looking up at me. Not knowing what I should do, I try to step back. "No," she says. So I don't. I keep holding her and we stand there. "I love you, Jaden. Maybe that's the wrong thing to say, but I always have. I said you should trust me, so I'm trusting you and I'm telling you. I love you."

Before he fell for Aspen, Sebastian didn't believe in love. I always wanted to—I just didn't know if I was worthy of it. But when she says it? This girl who can do anything? It's like a law. If she can love me, I must be worth something, right?

It's probably the wrong thing to do, but I answer her by putting my mouth to hers. I kiss her slowly, trying to show her exactly what I can't manage to say.

Her mouth opens and I dip my tongue inside. Then she does the same thing. My hand buries in her hair and hers knots in my shirt and she whimpers like she needs more of me. That one kiss travels the length of my body. My body is on fire in a different way now. A needy way. Priscilla stokes the fire as her mouth moves down my neck, kissing me there. I do the same to her, give and take, her then me. Her then me.

Stepping backward, I stumble into the room. We're still attached and still kissing. Right now, everything is silent. There's only her and me. This is different than any other time I've kissed her. Any other time I've done anything with any other girl.

When I move her shirt to the side to press my lips to her shoulder, she pulls away. "I'm sorry." The last thing I want to do is push her. I'm happy doing this.

But she only smiles at me and then hooks her hand in the bottom of her shirt and pulls it over her head.

Not going to lie, my eyes probably bulge out of my head. My shorts feel way tighter behind the zipper than they ever have to see her like this. Standing there in shorts and a purple bra against her skin. That she wants me—Jaden Sinclair, the fuck-up—to see her this way.

I'm frozen. It's embarrassing to admit I can hardly move as she lifts my shirt. I actually gasp when her hand brushes my skin, and then she pulls it over my head and tosses it to the floor. Open your mouth, Sinclair. Tell her this is a bad idea. Think with the right head. But it's so hard because she's so beautiful and this is the girl I've wanted forever. The girl I never thought could really, really want me back. "Priscilla, I don't know . . ." I want to shout the words and steal them back at the same time. Stab myself for taking the risk that she might agree, but proud of myself too.

"I do." And then she puts her hands behind her back to take off her bra.

My brain ceases to work. My body hums to life. A damn electrical storm is coming to life beneath my skin.

"I—"

She cuts me off. "I'm a big girl, Jaden. I know what I want." Her voice shakes a little, but in her eyes I can see she's serious.

I close my eyes. Right or wrong, there's no way I can walk away from this. From her.

My hands find her arms and gently pull them away from her bra. I can tell she's about to argue with me, but stops when I reach around her and close the sliding glass door.

I step behind her, push her hair out of the way, and kiss her shoulder. Little bumps pop up all over her skin. I kiss her again as my hands start to work the clasp on her bra. I open it, slide the straps down her arms.

I can't believe this is happening. That I'm here with her — like this.

I'm scared to death I won't be able to make it last.

When it drops to the floor, I step around her again. Look at her because there is absolutely nowhere else my eyes can be right now.

"*Dios*," Is the first word that comes out of my mouth, which is absolutely ridiculous. She's the one who talks Spanish, not me, but it's all I have.

She giggles nervously.

"You're beautiful," I tell her.

And then I lead her to the bed.

Priscilla's hand is on my bare chest, her head resting on my arm. We're laying here, quiet for what feels like ten years. I want to ask her if she's okay. If she regrets it, regrets me, but I'm too freaked out by what she might say, so I just hold her and stroke her and try not to concentrate on seeing her and what we did over and over in my head.

"Jaden?" she finally says after who knows how long.

"Yeah?"

"I . . . I want to tell you I'm sorry. All the times I call you names. When I say stupid or idiot. I don't mean it. Not really. It's just —"

"Hey. No worries. It's cool. I like it when I make you all feisty like that."

She doesn't laugh like I want her to.

"It's not right. I shouldn't have said it because you're none of those things. It's wrong and I'm sorry."

The things this girl does to me. I'm on fire here. I actually think I want to cry. I don't remember the last time I did that, and I won't let myself now, but she's so freaking incredible.

"I'm sorry, too. For almost kissing you at the party — actually, for not kissing you at the party. For being so weak this whole year. I should have trusted you. I do, I mean. It's just —"

"It's okay. just don't shut me out. No matter what, we're friends, Jay. Always."

More time passes and we lay there. I think about her clothes on the floor and her bare body under the blanket. More than that I think about all the laughs we've had and the fun. All the years we've known each other and all the good things that have happened. Of the way I would do anything for her and the fact that I think she would do anything for me too.

"Can I tell you something?" It's easier that I'm not looking at her as I speak.

"You can tell me anything."

I know. "I want New York. I don't want to go to Texas. I mean . . . who's the voice of reason if I leave you guys?" *How can I leave you?*

"Don't pretend to joke, Jay. Not now. And if you

want New York, come with us. You deserve to have anything you want. We'll make it work if that's what you really want."

I do. But can I have it?

She takes a few breaths and I know she's working up to something. Priscilla rolls onto her stomach and looks at me. "You know . . . if you wanted to go see your real dad, I would go with you. It might help. To talk to him."

I shake my head. "It won't." What I really mean is I can't. I can't risk seeing first hand that he doesn't want me either.

CHAPTER SIXTEEN

I'm still in shock for several reasons when I wake up the next morning.

I told Priscilla about my family. I haven't talked to anyone about it, ever. None of my best friends. Why not? The world didn't explode. I didn't. I actually might feel better.

And Priscilla. Holy shit. She loves me? Me? And we . . .

Stupidly, I freeze as though I'm doing something wrong when she stirs next to me. She snored last night, but it didn't matter. She's still the sexiest girl I've ever seen. I let my hand move up and down her back, watching as she gets goose bumps. Watching her dark skin flush.

I love her, too. I've always known it. Even when I didn't want to admit it.

"You're nothing." Mike's words come back, but that can't be true. I can't be nothing if she loves me.

When a knock sounds on the door, I jump out of bed. A condom wrapper crunches beneath my feet. Priscilla doesn't move. Knowing it's Sebastian,

I make sure she's covered up before I pull my shorts on.

I open the door only about three inches, not taking the chance he can see inside. "What's up?" I scratch my head and for some reason he's speechless.

Sebastian is looking at me all wide-eyed and shocked. "Holy shit!"

Holy shit? I push out the door and close it behind me. I have no idea how he knows, but he does.

"Holy shit!" he says again.

"Dude, shut up!"

He shakes his head. "I'm shutting, I'm shutting, it's just . . . Holy shit! I'm trippin' out here. You have a hickey on your neck!" I cover it like that will make him forget about it or something. "Seriously, Sebastian. I'm going to punch you in the mouth if you don't shut it. You better not say anything. I don't want her to be embarrassed."

"I won't. I'm not an idiot." He crosses his arms and I notice he's already dressed. I forgot we're supposed to leave Chicago today, which means it's early and Priscilla and I are behind.

All of a sudden, the shocked look on his face starts to morph into something different. He's serious when he looks at me and says, "If you leave now, you're going to break her heart, Jay. I love you, man, and you're like my brother, but I'll kick your ass if you hurt her."

I roll my eyes. "Whatever."

"I'm not playing around here. You wanted to do the same thing to me when it came to Aspen last year. I screwed up, don't do the same. It will be even worse now."

He's right. I lean against the wall and slide down it. He sits next to me on the floor. My feet are on the ground, my knees up with my arms resting on them and he's the same. "I won't hurt her. I'm gonna," I shrug, "I'm gonna do the New York thing. You have a roommate again." I hit him.

"Oh . . ."

"Oh? What do you mean, oh?"

"I just . . . I was going to stay with them. Pris and Aspen figured they could hide me in their place. It's not like Pris's parents will be out there much. I'm sure I could get it past Mom. Or hell, I could just tell her. She's not stupid and she wouldn't have to know Pris's parents would freak."

They're the ones who are fronting most of the money for their apartment. Aspen's parents were helping, but I'm pretty sure it's mostly Priscilla's gig and I'm pretty sure it's expensive too.

"No worries, though. I haven't told Ma yet so we can still get our place."

On the other side of New York.

"I don't want to screw things up if you want to stay with them." Like he doesn't want to live with his girlfriend?

"Shut the hell up." Sebastian holds out his fist. "It wouldn't have been the same without you."

For the first time in a while, I bump it.

I hold Pris's hand while we're sitting in the back of the Explorer. Aspen looks back at us about a million times the first couple hours and I can see the questions all over her face. I'm hoping there are answers to them.

I know I love her—but I haven't told her.

I know last night meant a lot to me—which I did tell her.

I know I want to be with her—but I still don't know if I deserve her.

I know I want New York—but I still don't know if I can make it work.

It's not like I've been real careful with my money on this trip. I wasn't planning on needing it for New York anymore. Will I be able to help Bastian with rent? Find a job? I'm scared I won't be able to find one, and I'm also freaked I will. I don't want to be the loser who's not in school when the rest of them are this Fall, but how will I swing that on such short notice, too?

And when she's there . . . with all those guys who are way better than me and actually making something of themselves, she'll realize even more that I'm nothing.

Priscilla squeezes my hand and drops her head onto my shoulder. "Stop overthinking. I hear the wheels turning over there."

I laugh because what else can I do? This girl knows me better than anyone.

Aspen looks over her shoulder again. Looks at our hands and Priscilla leaning on me and I see all the questions in her eyes. I have a feeling they're in desperate need for some girl time. Which, honestly, scares the Hell out of me. All guys are probably nervous about what is said about them during girl-talk.

But then I look down and see Priscilla smile at her and I wonder if she needs it, too.

"Sebastian, stop at the next gas station, yeah?"

About fifteen minutes later he pulls off the freeway and stops at a gas station. The girls climb out of the car and head straight to the bathroom together.

Sebastian nudges me. "You know they're in there talking about you, right?"

"Yeah, man. Thanks for reminding me."

"Got something to worry about?" He moves out of the way as I swing at him.

"Shut up." As far as comebacks go, it could use some work, but right now it's all I have. "Care if I sit up front with you? Let them do their thing if they need to?"

"Nah, it's cool."

He goes ahead and fills the tank while I run in and grab some munchies. The girls are standing with him when I come out.

"You wanna sit in the back with Aspen?" I lean over and whisper in her ear.

She gives me a huge smile and kisses me. "Yeah, Thanks."

I can't help but wonder what I did to deserve it.

"Girls!" Sebastian sings the lyrics to one of his favorite songs.

"Dude, what's White Castle?" Sebastian breaks off our rapping and lets the Beastie Boys continue.

"I think it's like a hamburger place? I don't know."

"Oh my God! Do you guys listen to anything but the Beastie Boys?" Aspen yells from the back seat.

At the same time we answer by singing about girls again.

Priscilla smacks me upside the head.

Aspen puts a knee in the back of Sebastian's seat and all we can do is laugh.

"You're way too young to like them that much." Priscilla rolls her eyes.

"I'm going to pretend you didn't say that."

Sebastian leans forward and presses a button on the CD player to play it again.

My laughter takes me over as Priscilla says from the backseat, "They're not allowed to sit up front together anymore."

The cool part is she sounds just as happy as me.

I don't know what makes me do it, but I try to call Mom when we're almost in New York. No one answers. Which shouldn't be a big deal, but for some reason, my gut sinks.

I've never seen anything like New York.

Nothing.

I've been to big cities. We just left Chicago, but we all lean forward in our seats as we get into the city. Lights, buildings, people.

"I can't wait to walk around Greenwich Village. I want to hear poetry and drink coffee." Aspen sounds in awe.

"I want to go see a Broadway Play," Priscilla adds. She likes plays, I realize. The one in Chicago, here, and she even dragged us to a couple at our high school.

"I so want to hit Times Square." This from Sebastian.

I'm actually not sure what I want to see or do. Even though I always planned to come out here with them, I wonder if I ever believed it would really happen? If I ever thought I would get a chance to see any of it?

"What about you, Jay? What do you want to do?" Priscilla says into my ear.

"I think I want to do it all."

Our first night in New York we head to a hotel. Priscilla is supposed to call the realtor tomorrow so they can meet and get the keys to their apartment. We're all tired, but we're in freaking *New York City* so there's no way we're staying in tonight.

And since it's a weekend in New York, what better place to hit than Times Square?

Priscilla is in the shower and I just got out a few minutes ago. I have on a pair of blue jeans, my black studded belt, and white t-shirt. As I'm pulling on the white short-sleeve button up to go over it, I hear the blow dryer in the bathroom.

Pulling out my cell, I dial home. It rings a million times and no one answers. Next, I try her cell, but get the voicemail and leave her a message.

Nausea eats at my insides, but I try to ignore it.

There's no reason for me to worry. They're probably off doing whatever it is they do. Having fun. Being happy. It's not as if she ever worried how anything affected me before, so why should I stress about her?

The blow dryer turns off and Priscilla steps out of the bathroom.

My mouth immediately goes dry as I take her in. It's nothing different than she would usually wear. A pair of tight jeans. A shirt that dips down in the front and has some tie thing below her breasts, but somehow it's different. Maybe just because we're different.

"Speechless?" She winks at me.

"Absolutely," I reply and then step toward her. I pull her into my arms and kiss her head. "You're gorgeous."

"You don't clean up so bad yourself."

When we pull away, I shove the cell back in my pocket.

"What were you doing?" she asks.

I'm about to tell her *nothing*. The words almost come out of my mouth without even thinking about it, but it doesn't feel right. Yeah, I'm totally turning over a new leaf or something.

"I tried to call my mom. She didn't answer. Didn't answer earlier either."

"Are you worried?" She hugs me.

I answer as truthfully as I can, "I don't know." I kiss her again.

"I'm sure everything's fine. I mean . . . he's never done anything, right? I mean—"

I tense. "I know what you mean. No. I wouldn't have left if he ever hit her or called her names or anything." Though that's not really true, is it? He started calling her names at the end. He'd called her a lot of names when he told me he wasn't my dad. No. I'm trippin' out. Overreacting. "I'm sure everything's fine." Her words come out of my mouth this time.

"We'll keep trying. I'll call, too."

"Thanks." I lean forward and take her mouth because it's the only thing I can think to do.

When we come up for air, she's biting her lip. Her eyes looking anywhere except on me. "Listen . . . I know you didn't want to talk about it last night, but I think we should. Or you should think about going to see your dad. You can probably get a lot of closure if—"

"No." I shake my head. The thought of seeing him gives me a lump in my throat. Makes a fist squeeze the breath out of me. "I can't. I know it's stupid, but I just can't."

Priscilla grabs onto me when I try to pull away. "It's not stupid, Jaden. It's a big deal. I get it."

Man this girl is awesome. I still don't get it. Why she chose me. Why she'd want me, but I'm stoked that she does. "Thanks." I let her hair slide through my fingers.

"For what?" she asks, confusion in her voice.

"For you." I'm sure it sounds stupid, but it's true. The glow in her eyes makes me wonder if maybe, just maybe, it wasn't stupid. If for once, it might have been perfect.

"Come on." My fingers weave together with hers. "Let's be the ones to knock on their door this time."

With that we head out to get our friends.

Times Square is freaking incredible. I've never seen anything like it. Even Sebastian is speechless which says a lot because he has a big mouth and always has something to say.

I don't even know what it is about the place. I mean, there're stores there, but there are stores everywhere. Pubs and bars we'd all do anything to get into. Museums and theaters Priscilla can't keep her eyes off. I can't get my eyes off her.

Sebastian's hands latched with Aspen's and mine with Priscilla's as we practically spin in a circle trying to take it all in.

This is going to sound totally lame, but I suddenly feel small. Not in a bad way, but in a normal way.

Like I'm just this person like everyone else and my problems feel so much smaller.

For the first time, I wonder if I might really be able to lose all my issues here. If I can make them get lost in the sea of people and lights and activity. If Priscilla can help me make them go away.

Like I said . . . Lame, right?

"This is so kickass." Sebastian finally finds his voice.

"For sure," I add.

We go into a music store and embarrass the girls by singing to them. Priscilla's brown skin highlights pink and it's seriously hot. When Sebastian breaks into a dance it's too much even for me. "Now you're embarrassing yourself. You can't dance for shit."

"You're just jealous of my mad skills."

The words are hardly out of his mouth before I pull him into a headlock.

"You guys are so embarrassing!" Aspen says before ducking down another row. Priscilla is right behind her.

"Aspen! Priscilla! Wait for us!" I tease loudly. A few people are looking at us and they're trying to get away.

By the time we stumble toward the door, we're getting way too many dirty looks from people and decide to make our way out. The four of us are laughing like crazy as we spill onto the street.

Next we have ice cream. Priscilla takes forever

to choose and finally I slip my arms around her waist from behind and say, "What's taking you so long? We know you're going to get strawberry like you always do."

Her Spanish accent is heavy when she says, "And you're just going to get chocolate, right?"

I smile even though it's the most cheeseball thing in the world to be happy about, but then I realize she won't care. Hell, she'll probably like it too, so I lean forward, my mouth right next to her ear. "Check us out. We're one of those couples who can order each other's ice cream and finish each other's sentence. We're the shit."

I'm rewarded for my killer sweetness by her turning enough to press her lips to mine.

"All right, enough of that, you two. There are children present." Sebastian tries to pull us apart.

"Quit messing with my game." I push him.

"Remember when I got with Aspen last year and you guys gave us so much shit?" He looks back and forth between the two of us. "Well, payback is a bitch."

We ignore him. I press a kiss to Pris's neck just to show him up.

We eat our ice cream and walk around some more. Really, it's just cool to be here. Cool to be here with them. A couple hours later as we're hailing a cab to go back to our room, I realize this is the only place

I should be. Actually it doesn't even have to be New York. It can be anywhere. I just need the people who are here with me right now.

Everything is perfect and I'm starting to believe it might really stay that way.

CHAPTER SEVENTEEN

W e're at breakfast the next morning when my phone rings. Everything inside me turns to ice. I don't know why. It's just my cell phone. It might be anyone, a wrong number or whatever, but for some reason, I have the sudden urge to puke.

My hands fumble with the phone and I see "Mom" light up on the screen. I have to swallow the bile in my throat as I push out of the chair and put the phone to my ear.

"What's wrong?" I ask. The words make me feel like crap because there shouldn't be something wrong because she's calling me. She's my mom and she's supposed to want to talk to me.

Too bad that's not the way it is.

A sob pierces my ear through the receiver. If I thought I felt cold before, it's nothing compared to the way I feel right now.

"Ja—den," she cries. "Mike . . ."

"What is it, Mom? What happened?" I try to make out when she's telling me as I head through the lobby so I can get back to our room.

A hand touches my shoulder and I don't have to turn around to know who it is. Maybe I should turn around though. Say or at least acknowledge her, but I don't. Mom is wailing at me. With each second dread slams into me harder. I'm a nail and it's a hammer beating my head over and over.

"Did he hurt you?" What will I do if he hurt her? It'll be my fault for leaving her. For not taking the brunt of his verbal assaults.

She's crying so hard I hardly understand her.

Priscilla and I are in the elevator now. My feet refuse to stay still as I pace the small space back and forth.

Don't let him have hurt her. Don't let him have hurt her.

Did she pray that same thing when he went off on me?

The sick feeling in my gut multiplies. I shouldn't be thinking about myself. Not right now.

"He's gone!" Her words are finally clear enough for me to understand. "He left me. He left me, he left me," she keeps mumbling over and over.

I actually exhale a sigh of relief. He's a bastard. Maybe things will be different for us now. Maybe she'll care about me when he's not around.

Mom cries again and that's when guilt hits for my thoughts. She loves him. Needs him, not me. "Are you okay?" I ask.

"No!" she yells. "He left me, Jaden! He . . . you . . ."

Her words are a whip lashing me with more strength than any of his could have. I just keep hearing the "you." It's my fault, it's my fault, it's my fault.

Why is everything my fault?

"How am I supposed to do it without him? What am I supposed to do now? I'm lost without him! What did you do? What *did you do*?" Then, she starts to wail and cry again.

I flinch. My eyes feel wet. What did I do? I don't know. But I have to fix it.

"Mom . . . I'm sorry."

I waver between guilt and anger. What could I have done? I'm here and she's there. *Why does it always have to be me*? But what if it is somehow my fault? Something I did, or because I left her there with him. Why did I leave her with him? "I'll be right there, okay?" I move around the room and start throwing stuff in my suitcase. "I'll fix it, okay? I promise. You stay there and I'll find a way to fix it."

She's crying so hard she doesn't answer. I don't know if it's the right thing to do, but I hang up the phone.

Scouring the room, I keep throwing things in the suitcase. Priscilla's on her phone. I can't hear anything she's saying over my pulse in my ears and part of me wants to ask her what she's doing, but the other part knows it shouldn't matter. Not when my mom needs me. I'm almost afraid to speak—scared that if I do I'll cry and the thought of crying in front of her makes me sick.

Next I move to the bathroom, throwing my toothbrush, deodorant, and everything else in my bag. When I come out Priscilla is off the phone and doing the same thing—gathering all her things and stuffing them into her suitcase. She's usually so careful by folding all her stuff, but this time it looks just as messy as mine.

"What are you doing?" It drives me crazy when I ask stupid questions. It's obvious what she's doing.

"Packing."

"Why?"

She looks at me, her eyes crinkled around the edges. "We have to go home, right? Your mom. I mean, it sounded like . . ."

Immediately I freeze up. This is my problem. Priscilla shouldn't have to go home because of it. I don't want her to see what I'm going home to. Don't want her to realize that I'm not worth it.

"You should stay here." I shrug as though it's not a big deal. "I mean, you guys are having fun, or whatever. You don't have to leave for me. I'm sure everything is okay." It's not, though. Or maybe it's just me who's not okay.

"It sounded like a big deal to me." Fire lights her words.

"That still doesn't mean you should have to go. Stay, have fun. You're supposed to get the keys to your apartment today, right?" I grab my bag, wanting the words back, but not having the balls to say so.

"*Dios*. Tell me you're not serious."

"Why wouldn't I be?"

Hurt flashes in her brown eyes. "You don't want me to go?"

I shake my head, imagining Priscilla coming home with me—hearing all the things they have to say. *You're nothing. It's your fault. Are you going to mooch off your friends forever?* "No. It's not that I don't want you to go, it's just . . . I don't need you to go." As soon as the words leave my mouth I know they're the worst thing I can say. The way she flinches is almost like I slapped her.

"That's not what I mean! It's not that I don't need you, it's just . . . you shouldn't have to go. You shouldn't have to pay for a plane ticket and all that for no reason. I'll be back soon." The words are like acid because though I want them, I don't believe them. How can I come back if Mom needs me there? What kind of person would I be?

"It's not for no reason." Priscilla crosses her arms. "It's for you."

For me. Is there anyone else who thinks about me the way she does? "I gotta go. It's not that big of a deal." Leaning forward I try to kiss her, but she pulls away.

Her eyes start to water, but I can see her fight it. See her jaw clench, making guilt bulldoze me. I'm already screwing up with her.

"Jaden, don't do this. Don't cut me out."

"I'm not!"

"Yes, you are! You don't think I could tell your mom was freaking out? You don't think I know this is hard for you? Why won't you let me be there for you? Do you not trust me? I can get Sebastian—"

"No! That's not what it is. I told you all that stuff."

"But when it matters, you still lock me out! Caring means being there for the good and the bad, Jaden. For both of us. You only want to let me in on the good."

"That's because you shouldn't have to deal with the bad! My shit shouldn't be your problem."

"When you love someone, their problems are always yours. It's not about giving someone graduation party because it looks good, but because you want to spend time with them. Or sending someone away, it's about being there."

I run a hand through my hair, not getting what

213

she's saying. And I don't have time for this. Not now. Mom needs me. And I need Priscilla.

"Don't hold it in. Let me be there for you, Jaden." The pain in her voice pulverizes my already shredded insides.

And I want her there. Want her there so much it makes my gut ache. More than that, I want what she's saying. I'm not sure if that makes me strong or weak, but right now it doesn't matter. I just want someone to have my back. Someone who is always there and not only for the good like she said or when they need me. Because even though I'm running off like this . . . I know Mom wouldn't do the same for me. And that kills me. But Priscilla? She would. She wants to.

"I can't keep doing this. I can't keep getting hurt by trying to be there when you don't want me. I do it with my parents and I can't do it with you, too."

She turns away from me and I know if I were to walk out the door right now, she'd let me. And she should. I don't want to hold it in. I don't want to do it alone. Maybe it makes me selfish or maybe it makes me the biggest fucking pussy in the world, but I want her there.

"Come with me," I blurt out. Funny, how I don't even try to be smooth with her. All I can be is real. "It's going to suck and I hate that you have to see it, or hear however I screwed up this time, but—"

214

Slowly, she turns and when she looks at me. Questions echo in my brain that I don't have answers to. That I don't want to even think about right now. Not how I will regret this or what she'll see or hear I just . . . "Come with me. Please."

Priscilla calls Sebastian and Aspen while we wait for a cab. They apparently tried to give us some space which really means, 'we-know-Jaden-is-freaking-out-and-he'll-be-embarrassed-if-we're-there'. Makes me feel all warm and fuzzy, let me tell you. Even my friends know I can't handle anything.

Then we get on the plane with tickets Priscilla bought while I'd been freaking out. I make her promise to let me pay her back.

My eyes keep jumping to her. My mind pulling up all kinds of scenarios for when we get home. Wondering what she'll think of me when Mom explains how I somehow screwed things up for her. Wasn't I supposed to make things better? By leaving she was supposed to be completely happy and now everything has somehow gone to shit and it's still my fault.

"You okay?" Priscilla grabs my hand.

"Yep."

"Obviously," she mumbles.

"Sorry. I don't mean to be a jerk."

Our flight only has one short layover. The closer we get to home the more edgy I get. I feel like I'm on something—all jumpy and twitchy.

We have to take a cab to my house. My mind is bouncing back and forth between Priscilla and Mom like someone passing a basketball.

What am I going to find when I get home?

What is Priscilla going to think?

Does Mom hate me now?

Do I want Priscilla to see whatever we find there?

The answer to that one is obviously no. "I was thinking . . . Maybe you should head home. I'll call you later and let you know how things go. I'm sure you don't want to deal with this crap."

Her head drops back against the back of the seat. "Do you not want me there or are you embarrassed? Or do you not think I want to be there?"

"Does it matter?" I scratch my head.

"Are all boys this dense?"

I let out a small laugh. "I don't know, Priscilla. I'm trying here."

"I know." Her head comes down on my shoulder. I love that she's like this with me now.

"I think I need to do this alone. Not because I don't trust you, but . . . I just think it's best."

"That's fine, Jay. I get it. Just don't shut me out. That's all I want."

"I won't. You're scary when you're pissed."

She pops up and smacks my leg.

"I'm kidding! I meant hot. You're way too hot to piss off."

We both start to laugh. Right as we pull up in my driveway she leans on my shoulder again.

"I'm serious."

"I know. I'll call you tomorrow. I promise."

CHAPTER EIGHTEEN

I seriously think there is something wrong with me. It seems like I'm always getting these strange feelings or thinking about stuff way more than I used to and I don't like it. I notice things more now, or maybe it's that I'm realizing what I notice? That makes no sense, but the second I step into the house, I feel like I don't belong here.

I was never really happy here. I never felt like it was mine, but it almost feels as though I'm trying to get into a foreign country without my passport. I made it over the border, but I'm prepared to get kicked out at any moment.

And for this particular vacation, it's forced so I'm actually kind of hoping to get the boot.

"Mike!" Mom's voice calls out as I close the door. "Mike, is that you?" She sounds frantic, her feet slapping against the hardwood floor as she runs round the corner. She slides to a stop when she sees me.

"Surprise!" I go for a smile. "But then, I guess it's not really a surprise since I told you I was on my way."

"Jaden." Her arms wrap around me and I find that I wanted it. Maybe needed it a little bit. I'm not sure what that says about me and right now I don't want to take the time to think about it. Or the fact that I'm shocked. She yelled at me on the phone, but she's hugging me?

"Hey, Mom. Are you okay?"

Her eyes are pink. Like maybe they were red, but she cried so much the color bled out.

She shakes her head and then her face is buried in my neck as she cries. The longer it lasts the more stressed out I'm getting. The angrier I am at him, freaked out he hurt her. All sorts of thoughts keep popping up in my head and I try to process them all.

"Come on. Let's sit down." We head into the living room and sit down. How can it feel so strange to be here after such a short amount of time?

"What happened, Mom?"

It freaks me out looking at her. She looks frail and sick. Is this for him? The man who treated me like shit my whole life? I don't get it.

"He's just gone, Jaden. I don't know where he went. It's been so hard ever since . . ." Her words trail off and she looks at her lap.

"Ever since what?" My body tenses because I have a feeling I know what she's going to say.

"Ever since you left he's been angrier. I keep

messing up. I need to get it together so I can make him happy again."

There has never been a moment where I hated Mike like I do right now. Hate him for making her feel like this. I grab her hand. "I'm pretty sure he's never happy unless he's tormenting someone, Mom. It's not you. It's not your fault."

She starts to shake. I don't get it. I don't understand how he can have this kind of effect on her.

"Yes it is. It's always been my fault. If I could give him what he needs, he wouldn't be so mad at me! I wouldn't force him to say such horrible things about me."

Bile rises in my throat and it feels like my chest is cracked open. "Screw that! You don't make him do anything. It's his problem, not yours. You don't need him in your life." *Need me.* Need your son.

She pulls her hand away and rubs her face. "He's been in my life since I was sixteen years old! He took care of me and protected me. You've never needed anyone, Jaden. I need him."

Her words make me lose my breath. I've never needed anyone? I feel like I need everyone, everything. I can't do anything on my own. And it would have been nice to have her . . .

"I'm nothing without him." She shakes her head. "Nothing."

My anger helps me find my tongue. "*He's* nothing! He's a bully. He lost his verbal punching bag and he took it out on you!" I push to my feet. "I'm sorry about that, Mom. I never wanted him to hurt you. I thought it would be better for you, but I can't handle hearing you talking about him like he's a king or something when he's treated me like crap my whole life."

"You don't understand!"

"No, I don't!" It's like she's programmed or something. She's depended on him. He's always been the most important to her, way more important than me, but I can't handle seeing her like this. Hearing her talk about how much she needs the man who called her a slut and shoved down my throat how worthless I am.

I feel like screaming. It seriously threatens to crawl up my throat. My body is ready to explode. She needs him? Him? "You let him treat me like shit! You let him hate me and never stood up for me!"

"Jaden." She shakes her head again before standing. She reaches for me, but I pull away. "It's not like that. I tried my best, by you. I loved you, but you have to think about how it made him feel. You were my mistake and he had to live with it every day. I had to live with it every day."

I flinch.

Somehow it makes her words register. "I didn't mean that. Not the way it sounded."

"It's okay." I take a couple steps backward. It's not okay at all, but I can't make myself say that. I was her mistake. I always reminded her of how she messed up. I ruined her life.

"Things were supposed to be better now," her voice breaks. "You were supposed to be happy there and we were supposed to be happy here. Why did you start in with him on the phone?"

So that's another way this is my fault. Right now, I can't feel, just react. "I didn't! It was him." It all makes sense. He needed someone to take his anger out on and I wasn't here, so he took it out on her. "I'm sorry, Mom."

That must be the wrong thing to say because she starts to cry again. I walk over to her and put my hand on her shoulder.

"I can't be alone, Jaden. I can't do it. I don't know how to be alone."

"You don't have to be alone, Mom. I'm here."

"You'll stay with me? You won't leave me alone?" she asks through sobs.

I want to say no. The thought makes everything inside me freeze—makes me feel lonely all of a sudden. I'm not supposed to stay here with her in this house I hate. I'm supposed to be in New York with my friends. With Priscilla. How can I leave her?

222

"Yeah, Mom . . . I'll stay. As long as you need me to, I'll stay."

My stomach is inside out as I drive Mom's car to Priscilla. My palms are sweaty. How am I supposed to do this? I mean, how can I leave her, after everything? Part of it is because I can't stand to let her down again. I know that's exactly what I'm doing. Will there ever be a time I'm not letting her down? Or someone down?

More than that, is it's me, too. I love this girl. She's freaking incredible. Everything about her is, and I'm the dumbass choosing to walk away from her? To leave her?

But it's for Mom.

Mom, who kicked me out.

Mom, who said I was a mistake.

I still can't get my head and heart on the same wavelength. After everything I've been through they're still not in sync and I wonder if they'll ever be. If I'll ever be.

My brain tells me to go, but it's that other part that's getting ripped apart. It wants to go, but feels obligated to stay.

Yeah, I'm totally screwed in the head.

"Hey," I say as she gets in the car. Turning sideways, I push a strand of hair out of her face and behind her ear. Her tongue sneaks out and licks her bottom lip. Her lashes are so long and dark, outlining her eyes. "You are so hot."

Priscilla returns my grin. "I missed you, too."

Once the car is in first gear, I pull away. Words bubble in my throat and I can't hold them back, not that I want to. "I did, you know. Miss you."

"I know."

We head to the park because we live in a lame town and there really isn't anywhere else to go. There's a little creek though and we sit by it just hanging out.

Tell her, tell her, tell her.

The words repeat in my brain, but it's another broken connection and I can't get them to come out of my mouth. Instead I keep on being afraid and lean back on the ground, my hands locked behind my head. Priscilla leans on my arm.

"You're quiet. Everything okay?" She reads me like she always does.

"Just the stuff with my mom. We got into it. She's really tripping out about my da—Mike. It's fucking crazy that I still forget and call him dad. It's not like he ever acted like one."

"It's a lot to take in, Jaden. You've gone through a lot of crap in a short amount of time. Give yourself a break, or I'll have to kick your butt."

"You can't kick nothing. I got mad skills."

"*Dios!*" She groans. "You just sounded like Sebastian."

"What? I'm way cooler than him. Plus, he'd say something dumb like ninja."

Priscilla laughs. "Because 'mad skills' is so much better than being a ninja."

"It is." I roll over and touch my lips to hers. Seriously. I've always liked kissing, but kissing other girls doesn't hold a candle to kissing her.

When we separate I look down at her. "She called me her mistake." I don't know why I feel the need to tell her. I feel kind of dumb, but I need to get it out too. Need to tell her.

"She doesn't deserve you." Priscilla's hand comes up and pushes my hair back. It fell into my face because of the way I'm leaned over. "None of them do. You're not a mistake, Jaden Sinclair."

"Thanks." And then because I feel like a total girl right now and I don't know what else to do with myself, I kiss her again. Still not man enough to use my mouth to tell her I have to stay.

"What the hell?" The car hardly comes to a stop in Mom's driveway, beside an all-too-familiar car, before I'm shoving out of the door and running to the house.

"Jaden!" Priscilla says, right behind me.

I stop. My breath rushes out, my heart pulse

slamming in my ears. Mike is here and I'll kill him if he hurt her, but I don't want Priscilla to have to deal with it.

"Here." I put Mom's keys in her hand. "Take her car, okay? I don't want you to have to hear this shit. I'll call you soon, baby."

Without waiting for her to reply, I head into the house. It feels like I'm having a heart attack. I can't make my breathing slow down and my heart is in my throat, but I can't stop picturing her yesterday: the tears and the pain in her voice and it's making me crack and break inside.

"Mom!" I rush into the kitchen and stumble, I'm so shocked at what I see. Which is nothing. It's normal, I mean. As if it's a regular day. Like she wasn't crying because he left her, because he made her feel unworthy. As though she didn't plan for me to help her. Stay with her.

If I thought I was losing it before, I'm literally going insane. How can she hang out with him in the kitchen like nothing happened?

"The prodigal son returns. Pretty little boy like you not man enough for the big bad world?" Mike sets down his spoon. He's sitting at the kitchen table, eating whatever the hell it is she cooked for him, after everything that happened?

I hate that I'm mute. I can't open my mouth and

fucking speak. My eyes dart to Mom as she stands by the stove, looking at me. Is she scared? Worried? Maybe both. I can't tell, but she's looking and not saying anything. Why am I surprised?

But then . . . I feel something at my side. Pris's hand on my arm and it pulls me out of my trance. "Actually, I was doing pretty well for myself before I had to come home and clean up your mess. Couldn't handle not picking on someone so you had to take it out on her when I left?"

His face pales. Hate lights his eyes. Yeah, obviously he doesn't like being called out in front of Priscilla. Well, I don't either. His jaw tenses. I can see it in his eyes, see him trying to calm himself so he doesn't react in front of her.

"Mom, let's go." I'm not sure where I plan to take her, but I'll get her out of here.

Each second drags out like a freaking year or something, but she's still not replying.

"Mom."

Priscilla's hand squeezes my arm. It reminds me I'm not standing here alone. Man, I didn't realize how much I need that.

"Jaden . . . I . . ." She looks at Mike, as though she needs his permission to speak.

"You what! Let's go! He left you. You don't need him."

"You little piece of shit." Mike pushes out of the chair so hard it falls to the floor. At the same time, I go for him. Priscilla holds onto me, her nails biting into me as Mom reaches for Mike.

"Jaden, let's just go, okay? Come on. We'll get our stuff and go back to New York."

"Don't let him do this, Mom. Don't let him keep breaking you down like this." My throat is scratchy.

"She's not going anywhere, you punk. She's mine. She belongs to me! Now you can shut your mouth and get the hell out of my house!"

"She—" I start, but Mom cuts me off.

"Jaden, it's okay. I want to be here. Everything is okay now. I'm okay. You can go."

With that I completely stop fighting Priscilla's hold. I stop moving. I might even stop breathing.

Mike jumps in, "Don't explain anything to him. He doesn't deserve to know. Coming in my home and insulting me."

I was willing to stay here for her. I flew all the way back for her. And it's still not good enough.

Without a word, I turn and walk out. Priscilla is with me.

No matter what, Mom will always love Mike more than me.

I get outside and realize I don't have a car. I got

us stuck here in the middle of a burning hot day without a car.

"Jaden, I . . ." Pris starts.

I shake my head. "I can't. Not right now." But then I grab her hand right as the screen door slams behind us.

It's Mom. With my stuff.

"Jaden, I'm so sorry. He came home and he apologized. It'll be okay now."

I don't even want to reply anymore. There's no use. No purpose. It won't make a difference.

"I love him, Jaden."

And there's the difference. She loves him. Not me. Not enough at least.

She hands me my bag and I take it. "We're taking the car. I'm not letting Priscilla walk. You can go get it from her house."

"Okay. I'll call you soon. Once things blow over, I'll call you."

Translation: don't call her. And I realize, I won't. Not anymore. I can't fix this. Never could. I flew all the way home to take care of her and it's still not enough.

"No, Mom. Don't call. You made your choice."

I squeeze my girl's hand. Ignoring the rock that landed on my chest, we walk away.

CHAPTER NINETEEN

"Are you okay?" Priscilla asks as we drive away. My hands pinch tightly around the steering wheel. My eyes hurt, and my chest aches. No, I'm not okay at all. I feel like going wild, crazy, doing anything to let out all the anger and pain trapped inside me.

"No."

"That was a stupid question. I'm sorry I asked." She reaches over and puts her hand on the back of my neck.

"I can drop you off at home, or whatever. I'll leave the car there and maybe go to Courtney's and we can figure out getting back to New York."

I think about what Mom said . . . What I said. I'd been willing to stay for her and hadn't even told Priscilla. That has to hurt her. The most important thing to me and I managed to hurt her again. I hate it.

"You're not getting rid of me, Jaden. We both go to Courtney's or we both go to my house."

"How is that going to work when your parents hate

me?" How many people are on that list now? The people that hate me. Must suck to be the one with the boyfriend you can't bring home.

Priscilla sighs. "They're not home, Jay. They don't even know I'm here. Mom had called me and told me they were going out of town for a week."

"I thought . . ." *They had to stay home for a while.* I stop when I realize what I was about to say. Smooth move, Sinclair. Leave it to me to almost mention something else that would hurt her.

"You thought right. I know they said they couldn't do any traveling for the next couple months—that's why they aren't coming out like Aspen's parents are."

Even more anger pulses inside me. How can they not realize how freaking amazing she is? How can they not want to spend more time with her? "We're quite a pair, huh?" I pull over in front of her house. Leaning over the center console, I pull her to me. "You're worth more than that, Priscilla. You're worth everything and they're insane not to know how special you are."

Tears glint in her eyes and I wipe them away. "I love you," I tell her. More tears start to pour out of her eyes. "I'm sorry. Is now not the time to say that? Should I go back to just telling you how hot you are?"

She smiles like I hoped she would, but she's still

crying when she says, "Now's the perfect time. I love you too."

We get out of the car and head into her house. It's huge. Like five of mine—my old house, I mean. There's a crystal chandelier hanging in the entry way and that's just the beginning. I've seen her house before, of course, but it's different now.

"It's so fake in here. Just like everything else, it's all for show."

Like always, she says the perfect thing.

"Do you want to talk about your mom?" We pass the formal living room and sit on the white couches in the family room.

"No. I don't even want to think about it right now. I just can't." Maybe I should. Maybe that makes me weak, but I can't help it. It's so much easier to process things inside than out. My brain works better than my mouth when it comes to stuff like that.

"Okay. I'm going to go take a shower then. You want to watch TV? Then we can make plans to go back to New York?"

"Can I join you, instead? That sounds like a lot more fun." I pull her to me. My hands rest on her hips and her arms come up around my neck. Her lips meet mine halfway and I kiss her. I know how her lips move now, how she likes to explore my mouth the same way I like to do to hers. When I pull away,

I'm thinking there's a pretty good chance she's about to tell me no, but when I start to follow her, she puts a hand on my chest.

"Don't even think about it, big guy."

I groan as she walks away, shaking her hips more than she usually does.

"Hey!" I call to her when she gets to the stairs. Priscilla stops and looks at me. "Thanks."

She might have nixed the shower idea, but I know she's only going up there to give me time to think. Because she knows I'm much better at that then talking about it.

"Any time."

She's not upstairs five minutes when I hear the door rattle. The sound does the same thing to my insides. It's her parents and they're totally going to freak when they see me. I know it. Before they might have tolerated me, but after the jail thing, I know things are different.

My first instinct is to run, but I stop myself. What kind of man would I be if I ran out? If I can't even man-up to her dad?

The door creaks open, then slams.

"I can't wait to get these clothes off you," a woman's voice says, all seductively.

Now I'm really freaking out because the last thing I want is to see her parents going at it.

"I can't wait for you to do it either, *señorita*."

The voices are getting closer and I start to look for a place to hide, hoping they'll end up upstairs.

I know I'm screwed when her dad stumbles around the corner and then a woman. Who most certainly isn't Priscilla's mom. Holy shit.

"Oh, shit." Pushes out of my mouth before I can stop it. What a bastard. How can he do this to Pris's mom? To Priscilla?

"What the hell are you doing in my house!" He jerks away from the woman, as though I don't know what would have gone down if I wasn't here. This asshole—the one that never has time for his daughter, but expects her to be perfect. Who only makes time for her when it will look good for him in public. The one who didn't even want me to come to her graduation party yet he's about to get busy with another woman in their house?

I forget about Mom.

About Mike.

About anything except for making it better for her. "I'm here with your daughter—with my girlfriend—who you're about to wreck."

His face goes pale. Dude, I swear I can see the wheels turning in his head, see him think and plot how to get his slimy ass out of this. I'm not even good enough to be her friend, yet he does this? His eyes dart to the stairs. She's still not there. The woman next to him is smiling and I can tell she's probably loving the fact that he got caught and thinking he'll really be hers now.

He pushes his hand in his pocket and pulls out his wallet. "How much?"

It's dumb, but his words don't register at first. "Huh?"

"You heard me. How much? What's going to keep your mouth shut about this?"

Anger erupts inside me. Anger for Priscilla. For her mom. At this prick standing in front of me. The one who everyone in town treats like a king and who makes his daughter feel like crap. The one who thinks he can buy me off when I just told him Priscilla's my girl. "You think I'll keep your secret for you for money? Hell no. She's way more important to me than any amount of money."

The jerk has the nerve to laugh. "You think I don't know who you are? Sinclair, you've been leeching off my daughter for years. I kept you out of trouble when you assaulted your dad. Why not take the money and run now?"

His words make me flinch. They weasel their way into me the same way he accuses me of doing with Priscilla. They're so close to what I've heard my whole life. What I see because everyone obviously keeps walking away from me.

"She'll never know. You can take the money. You need help with college, right? I can do that. You want to disappear for a while? I can help you with that, too. Hell, keep dating her if you want, because it will not last, but do yourself a favor, kid, and keep your mouth shut. She'll end up hating you for telling her—for breaking her heart and messing up her family. Do you want that? Want to make her hate you?"

But then, some other thoughts start to push in too. I have no doubts he could make all those things come true, but I don't want it. "There is nothing, *nothing* I wouldn't do for Priscilla. I don't give a shit about her money. I don't want it. Don't need it. The only thing I care about is making sure she's okay, which obviously you couldn't care less about."

And that makes me someone. That makes me more than her dad sees when he looks at me. It makes me more than he is. More than a lot of people would be. It makes me a good friend. A good boyfriend. A good person.

"I don't want your money. She means more to me than that and she deserves to know the truth. Jesus, do you know what kind of pressure you put on her? How you make her think she has to be perfect. And all you are is a liar and a fake."

"Who has a whole hell of a lot more friends and power than you do, kid."

But it doesn't matter. Do I think people would believe him over me? Yep. Do I think he could cause problems for me? Absolutely. Is it more important than her? Hell no.

How many times has Priscilla told me it doesn't matter what other people think? That Mike's problems or Mom's problems were theirs and not mine? The man standing in front of me is what everyone thinks they want to be—he's the kind of man I would have thought I'd want to be, but in this moment, I'd rather be like me than him.

Views are so freaking skewed—the way people see each other and the way they see themselves. Anything can change them or alter them. What you see on the outside usually isn't what you get on the inside and that's what matters. Actions. What you put out into the universe or whatever.

Right now I feel like more of a man than I ever have.

"I don't care what you do to me. How much you threaten me." Now, it's me walking closer to him. I won't let him back me down. "The girl upstairs is all that matters. And that sure as hell isn't taking your money and keeping my mouth shut so you can do what you want."

Mike hates me, and why? Because of something I had no control over. Nothing I ever would have done would be enough for him, and why? Because his ego couldn't handle the fact that once, even for one night or one hour, Mom wasn't under his thumb.

That isn't my fault. It doesn't say anything about me.

I know Mom doesn't hate me, but I think she might hate herself. Does that hurt? Yep, but I can't control it. I can't stop her. She's made her choices. They were never mine to make and I can't stop her or change her mind.

It's not my fault.

The man standing in front of me is a selfish liar. He doesn't want me around his daughter because of his skewed freaking vision of what is important.

Not my fault.

And I don't want to be like him.

How they see me isn't my fault. How could I have not realized this before?

I would do anything for Priscilla, Sebastian, Aspen. For Courtney, or even for Mom. I would have even walked away from Priscilla. I'm damn proud of that person.

And no one will make me walk away from Pris again.

"I don't care what you think of me or what you offer me. I care about Priscilla and how I'm going to go up to her room and break her heart because of you."

"You don't have to do anything. I heard it all." Pris walks down the stairs, her head held high.

"Priscilla. We need to talk." Her dad steps toward her, but my girl holds up her hand. All brave and strong in a way I never used to be.

"We don't need to do anything." She stops right in front of him. "How long?"

My feet carry me toward her. I stand behind her because I know she can do this on her own and because I want her to know I'm here if she needs me. I'll always have her back.

"Now isn't the time, Priscilla." His whole stance has changed. He's nervous and stiff.

"Now is the only time!" she yells and then looks at the woman who doesn't look so smug anymore. "How long?"

"A year and a half."

Priscilla flinches, but keeps going. "Was she the only one?"

"Don't demand answers from me, young lady."

"Was. She. The. Only. One?"

A slight shake of his head is the only answer she needs.

"Did you know you never made me feel like I was good enough? That I never would be unless I became like you? I don't want to be anything like you. Nothing. And Jaden is more of a man than you'll ever be."

There's a slight shake in her voice and I can tell she's not going to be able to hold it together much longer. I step forward and grab her hand.

"Are you ready to go?"

She looks at her dad one last time. "Yeah . . . yeah, I'm ready."

With that we walk outside, straight past Mom's car. I don't need it. Don't want it. We walk silently until we get to Courtney's. As soon as we step onto the porch, Pris loses it. I wrap my arms around her and hold her. "I'm sorry. So fucking sorry, Priscilla." The words keep coming out over and over. "I love you."

When the tears finally ease up, she wipes her eyes, before zeroing them in on me.

"Do you know how incredible you are, Jaden Sinclair? How rare you are? How good a person you are?"

I look at her and smile, "Yeah. I'm learning that. I really am." And I do. For real. I see who I am and though I'm not perfect, I like what I see.

The second we get to the baggage claim in New York, Sebastian is coming right for us.

"About time you guys got back! We were worried."

I laugh at him. "Dude, you sound like your mom."

"Sebastian! Get back in here! Give them some

space or time or something," Aspen yells from behind him.

"There's always time for me!" He tosses back at her before stopping and staring at us. I can tell he wants to ask us a million questions, that he's wondering what went down, but he doesn't do anything but stand there. For Sebastian's big mouth, that is huge.

"What are you guys doing here? We could have taken a cab back by ourselves," Priscilla asks, but I just shake my head. I'm not surprised at all. I know she's not really, either.

"Dude! We didn't know what happened. Just that you guys went home." He shrugs. "We needed to make sure things were okay, or whatever."

I don't mention that since we're back, everything is obviously okay. It's cool he cares.

He's a nutcase. Obnoxious. Loud. But he's my best friend. A kick ass friend, who I'm honored to have and who probably thinks the same thing of me. Especially the obnoxious part.

"You just didn't want to miss any excitement."

"No shit. That's a given."

Aspen punches his arm. "Bastian! You're so bad."

"That's not what you said last—ouch!" he says as she hits him again. "I'm sorry, baby. You're right. I'm bad and you're awesome. Just don't hit me again."

Then we're all quiet and I know they know something big went down. There are hundreds of people around us in the airport. People run into us, but it doesn't matter. I'm glad they're here. All of them. I hold out my fist and Sebastian bumps it.

"*Dios!* Enough with the stupid boy stuff." Priscilla puts one arm around me and the other around Aspen. Aspen returns Priscilla's hold and then puts her other arm on Sebastian. Without a word, he and I complete the circle. A tight, unbreakable circle. We probably look like idiots, but I don't care and I'm sure they don't, either.

How could I not have known I have everything I need right here? That these people wouldn't be my friend if I wasn't as incredible as they are?

I'm awesome. Does it sound cocky? Yep, but it's true.

I'm awesome because of them and they just might be the way they are because of me.

I have a girl I love.

I have my friends, who I love as well.

Courtney and Roger and maybe even the person who lives on the address in my pocket. One day, I might go there. Or not. I don't think it really matters. I know who I am. These people know who I am. I have everything I need right here.

"I hope this doesn't mean we plan on hugging all the time, Jay. I mean, you're my boy but . . ."

"You're so stupid." I shake my head. "You're my boy too, but you're definitely not pretty enough to keep hugging."

But none of us let go right away.

I remember something Sebastian said before. Something I rolled my eyes at, at the time. "A package deal."

"All for one, or whatever," he adds.

EPILOGUE

"New York is way too freaking cold in the winter." I blow on the coffee in my hand. My gloved hand. Priscilla is sitting next to me in the brown leather booth.

"It's not that bad. You're such a baby."

"Your baby." Leaning over I nuzzle her neck. I don't even care that the words are cheesy. I would have made fun of Sebastian for saying them a few months ago. I would probably still make fun of him if he said the same thing, just for a laugh. It's different when I say stuff like that though.

"I don't know whether to roll my eyes at you or swoon."

I love that my girl speaks her mind and is tough as nails. So hot.

"How about you roll your eyes now just because you're sexy when you're frustrated and you can swoon when we're alone?"

This really makes her roll her eyes and I even get a swat on the arm for it. Totally worth it.

Priscilla, Sebastian and Aspen are all on winter

break from school. We went home for a bit, but came back because school starts again in a few days. For all of us. It'll be my first semester and I'm only taking a few classes, but I'm cool with that. I'll owe a ton in loans when I'm done, but I'm cool with that, too. Feels good that I'm going to start at all, and that I'm doing it on my own, so the rest of it doesn't matter. I'm thinking Engineering.

"What time do you work tomorrow?" I kiss her neck. She works at this coffee shop. Loves it. Her dad wasn't too happy about it, but she doesn't really care what he's happy about. She's who she is and he can take it or leave it. Her mom seems pretty proud though. And she comes out to visit often, too. Their divorce will be final in a few weeks, I think.

"Nine. Listen, are you sure you want me here, Jay? I totally understand if you want to do this by yourself. I mean, you're meeting your dad for the first time. I don't want to intrude."

I pull my face out of her neck and look at her. "You never intrude." Pushing her hair out of her face, I tuck a strand behind her ear. "I need you here."

She cocks her head. "You don't need me, Jay."

"Fine, then I want you here. I know I can do it on my own, but I don't want to."

"Are you nervous?"

"No. Yeah. Kind of. I mean, it's a big thing, ya

know?" I called him for the first time mid-September. Seriously hard, let me tell you.

But he didn't know about me. He'd never known. I knew him and my mom were young and I don't even know how she still knew where he was or found him again to give me the info, but what matters is he never didn't want me—he didn't know I was out there.

We've talked for over three months. Every friggin' week. He calls a lot. He's an architect. Loves old buildings and his wife said he takes half the stuff around their house apart all the time. Apparently he's not as good as me at putting it back together again.

I'm the man, what can I say?

"It's a huge thing. I totally understand. You'll be great though, and he'll love you."

I think about all our phone calls. All the things he's said to me. How he's wanted to meet me from the first day I called him, but waited until I was ready. I offered to come to him, but he wouldn't have it. He wanted to come to me. No one in my life but my four best friends and Sebastian's mom have ever given a shit about me like that.

It feels awesome.

"He already does, Priscilla. I think he already does." And if things don't work out, I'll still be okay. I don't need anyone else to prove to me who I am.

She leans forward and kisses me.

"What was that for?"

"For being you . . . and because you're hot."

I wink at her. "Well, we know that."

"I love you."

"I love you, too."

"Jaden?" A voice says from next to the booth. I look over to see my dad. My real dad. His hair is light brown like mine. And he's smiling.

"Umm . . . yeah. Hey. It's me."

I stand up and he pulls me into a hug and cries. Tension seeps out of my body.

It's at this moment I realize Priscilla and I have exactly what we wanted. With or without him, we're exactly what we wanted to be . . . happy. Having a dad is a pretty cool bonus, though. I can't wait to see just how cool it can be.

Read on for a taster of the companion novel to
What A Boy Needs . . .

WHAT A BOY WANTS

CHAPTER ONE

There was nothing better than opening my email to a job offer. Well, I could think of a few things I liked more, but money wise, this topped the list. Another love-struck girl, in desperate need of my services. And another hundred bucks in my pocket. Sweet!

To: Hook-up Doctor <hookup_doctor@yahoo.com>
From: PA Rocks <icantbelieveididthis@yahoo.com>
Subject: Boy help?
Dear Mr. Hook-up Doctor,

I snorted. Mr. Hook-up Doctor? That was a first. I'd been at this for six months now, and I had yet to be called Mr. anything.

I kind of liked it.

Maybe I'd start using it from now on. It made my business sound more legit. Like I was one of those guys in a suit, sitting in a high-rise office in some big city, instead of a broke, seventeen-year-old with no wheels. I could definitely get used to that fantasy.

Except . . . I'm not really a suit kind of guy. It would be my high-rise office, though. I could wear whatever the hell I wanted. I was thinking jeans and t-shirts as the required uniform. Oh, and Vans. Have to have the Vans.

I twisted the ring in my eyebrow and looked down at my laptop again. I could figure that crap out later. My fundage was running low, and an email to my Hook-up Doctor account meant possible money. Money meant a car. Cars equaled more chicks. You get the picture.

Mr. Hook-up Doctor,

Umm, yeah. This is weirder than I thought it would be. I'm sure you get that a lot. I'm really not like the other girls who need your help, though. Well, not that I know any girls who have come to you, but I'm not the kind of girl who usually does something like this. Ugh! I'm rambling, aren't I?

"No, shit. What was your first clue?" I groaned.

Okay, sorry. I'm just not used to emailing someone to get a guy. I'm the sensible one. I don't need someone to help me with boys.

Not that I'm a compulsive dater or anything, and well, I guess it's obvious I need help since I'm emailing you, but this is different. What I'm trying to say is, I'm not the kind of girl who would usually give a guy who wasn't into her the time of day. Damn, I'm rambling again. Sorry.

I don't really know what kind of information you need, so yeah, I'll end this painful email. I just wanted to see if you're available to help. This guy, well, he's kind of out of my league. Not like he thinks he's too good for me, it's just . . . yeah, he's not the kind of guy who dates a girl like me. Can you help? What's the next step? Your blog isn't really too forthcoming on information, you know.

Hope to hear from you soon!

PA Rocks (This whole process is confidential, right?)

Shaking my head, I leaned back in my computer chair and kicked my feet up on the desk. Pulling a dart out of the arm of my chair, I tossed it at the dartboard on my wall.

See? This was a classic example of why girls don't get the guys they want. We don't like that wishy-washy,

253

back and forth crap. Girls need to decide who they are: either the strong, confident chick who puts us on our ass and still makes us want more, or the shy girl next door who we want to either corrupt or bring home to our parents. A toss-up.

Or, there were those girls in between. When I say in between, I don't mean they're all over the place like PA, but they're not the man-eater girls or the completely innocent ones, either. They know who they are. They're confident in a more quiet way. They're subtle, not pushy like Black Widow Girl or too standoffish like Little Miss Innocent, they're . . . cool.

Unfortunately, you don't run into the latter girl too often. And honestly, when guys do, a lot of the time we don't notice her. Sucks, but true.

I threw another dart at the board. My finger lingered over the mouse. Without letting myself think too much about it, I hit reply.

Miss PA,

I usually don't do this, but I'm going to give you a small piece of free advice. Then, we can talk details and see if you want to go through with this. I can tell you right now why you don't have the guy you want. Make up your mind about who you are. Half the email you were all, I-am-woman-hear-me-roar. And the rest of the time, you were the unsure chick who stumbles over her words and hides in the corner of the gym during the dances. We're guys. Half the time, we don't know who we are. It helps things become a lot easier if we know who you are.

I can hear you now, and before you go all She-Woman on me, let me tell you, I know it's a double standard. I will fully admit crap like that goes on. You know, the whole "life's not fair" thing. Nothing we can do about it. I didn't make the rules, I just know them.

That advice was free. I usually don't do that (a guy has to make money). From now on, everything costs.

Anyway, yes, this is confidential. I don't want anyone knowing who I am any more than you do (hence the whole 007 email thing).

My services are a hundred bucks. I know that seems like a lot, but you're trying to score your dream guy here. I'm worth it. I promise. I take fifty dollars up front and fifty after. You don't pay the last fifty if you don't get the guy (it's never happened). I'll give you instructions later on how to pay. What I need you to do is decide if you want to continue. If so, I really need you to think about which of those girls you are and let me know. Each of my clients get a personalized plan of action, so I need to know about who you are and a little about the guy. No names. Make up some kind of code name for him (please, no hottie, cutie etc. A guy can only take so much). I don't need to know his date of birth, hair color and favorite thing to do on a first date or anything. I'm talking basics here.

Hope to hear from you soon.

Hook-up Doctor

Pushing out of my chair, I pulled my t-shirt over my head and tossed it into the pile of clothes next to my guitar. One clean shirt later, I was out the door, jogging down the stairs, and hoping to make it out of the house before—

"Sebastian Dale Hawkins! Where are you going? I told you Roger was coming over tonight. He really wants to meet you." *Shit.* The full name and everything.

My mom walked around the side of the stairs, crossed her arms and glared at me, still wearing her "Courtney's Dance Studio" shirt. Yes, my mom taught dance, but not the sleazy kind. If I had a dollar for every time someone made a wise crack about it, I wouldn't need to be The Hook-up Doctor at all.

"Ma, why does he want to meet me? I mean, it's not like I'm five years old and looking for a daddy." I might sound harsh, but it was always the same thing. She met a new guy and we had to play house. After seventeen years, I was pretty sick of it.

"Because he's a nice guy? Because we're in a serious relationship, and you're my son? Come on, Sebastian. I really think he might be the one." My mom's bottom lip poked out like she was a toddler trying to get her way. Or, hell, maybe that was just a girl thing. I'd file that bit of information away for later. Might be something I could use as The Hook-up Doctor.

I had to say, she knew what she was doing. My mom was good. For teaching people how to get what they want, I obviously learned from the best. But after a while, I also learned how to say no to her. "I can't. You know I would, but I have this project I have to work on with Aspen. I'm heading over there right now."

"Why are you going there? I know she'd rather be over here than snacking on tofu burgers at her house."

It's hard to bullshit a bull-shitter. By the way Mom narrowed her brown eyes at me, I knew she wasn't buying what I was trying to sell her. "I'm going over there, and then she's driving me to meet up with Jaden and Pris. It's a group . . . project . . . thing." She gave me those all-knowing eyes that made it hard to lie to her.

"Next time?" she pleaded.

"Sure." I let the lie roll off my tongue. I had no desire to meet this guy. What was the point? The four husbands before him weren't the one, and I doubted he was either. Still, I pulled her into a hug, because I knew she'd just let me off the hook on purpose and yeah, I'm a guy and I love my mom. So shoot me. I'm man enough to hug her without feeling like a mama's boy.

After a quick squeeze, she finally let me go. "Oh, and, Sebastian? It's Friday night before the last week of school. Going out with your friends would have been a more believable excuse than a group project thing." My mom winked at me.

I'm an idiot.

I pulled on my Vans and slipped out. It took me about thirty seconds to walk two doors down to Aspen's. Her house was the only one on the block painted a different color. Her front door was orange. Who would do that?

I raised my hand to knock, but her mom pulled it open before my fist came in contact with the door. And here was the very person who would have an orange front door.

"Come in, Sebastian. Phil's meditating," she whispered, and I fought some serious eye-rollage. "Sneak upstairs. Aspen is in her room—unless, you need to be centered? I'm sure Phil wouldn't mind if you joined him." She smiled all hopeful-like and I really hated to deflate her excitement, but not as much as I disliked the idea of being centered.

With a shake of my head, I tip-toed up the stairs, realizing I should have gone to her window. Her room faced the backyard, and their gate was always unlocked. Aspen has begged me a million times to hike the side of the mountain that was her house, instead of using the front door. I think her parents embarrassed her, and I could see why, but it always felt too *Dawson's Creek* for me. The fact that I knew a show that had been off the air for years well enough to know climbing through her window was too Dawson/Pacey-like, made the whole window thing an even bigger hell no. I blamed it on that Katie chick marrying Tom Cruise. I might have to start rethinking the Spiderman thing if it came down to finding my inner feng shui or climbing a damn trellis.

Aspen's door was half open, so instead of knocking, I slipped it open slowly, pulled some more twinkle-toe walking like I'd done on the stairs and grabbed her shoulders. "Boo!"

"Ahh!" She jumped, slammed her laptop closed and whirled around, her honey-brown ponytail flying out and almost poking me in the eye. She gave me that pissed-off Aspen look, and I knew I was screwed.

"What the hell, Sebastian! You scared the crap out of me."

Yeah, I knew I was a punk, but I couldn't help it. I laughed. "That was classic. You looked like you were going to pee your pants." She punched me in the arm, and I laughed louder.

"Shut up." She leaned backward against her desk, with a hand on her laptop.

"Don't pout, Woodstock. You can't help that I'm stealthy as a ninja."

She pushed past me, bright green eyes throwing daggers my way as she picked her cell phone up off the bedside table. I ignored her dirty looks and flopped down on her bed, kicking my feet up on the purple comforter. "We should probably wait a few minutes before we bail. Daddy Peace is meditating, and your mom already tried to get me to do it, too. I'm sure she wouldn't let you escape quite as easily as she did me."

"See! That's why I tell you to come in the window. All you had to do is climb that lazy butt of yours up the side of the house, let me know you were here, and then I could have snuck out. Now she'll be watching for me." Aspen sat down at the foot of her bed. She was a t-shirt and jeans kind of girl, but when she leaned over to tie her shoes, I caught a glimpse of smooth, creamy skin right above her jeans that had me wondering for the first time what she'd look like if she decided to show a little more flesh every now and again.

I didn't *like* her because—well, I didn't really do the whole "like" thing. I did the fun thing, and I didn't think Aspen would be down for that. There were way too many chicks in the proverbial sea to ruin a friendship for a sliver of skin, anyway. "Oh, I see. So I have to scale your house, and you get to sneak out the front door?"

"Now you're getting it. See how smart you are?" she teased back.

"Aw, you think I'm smart? That's so nice of you to say." I crossed my arms, waiting for her next comeback.

"No, I think you're cocky."

"Yeah, that's what's Stephanie said, too—ouch!" I covered the family jewels as she attacked me with her other shoe. "Settle down, woman. You're violent!" I chuckled as her dainty little shoe hit me in the thigh.

"Men," she mumbled. "I've had about enough of conceited guys today."

She stopped hitting me, and I sat up next to her, nudging her with my shoulder. "What's wrong, Woodstock?"

She used to hate it when I called her that, but over

the years, she'd gotten used to it. I couldn't help it. Her parents were tree-hugging hippies. Not that I had anything against that, but they were always telling us stories about their peace and love adventures. They're not old enough to have gone to Woodstock or anything, but it made for easy jokes.

"Nothing."

She tried to stand up, but I pulled her back down by the wrist. I gave her crap, but if any other guy did it, I'd kick his ass. If he was bigger than me, Jaden would help, too. That was what our group did. We always backed each other up. "Seriously. Did something happen?"

Her cell phone beep cut off our conversation. Aspen flipped it over. "It's Jaden." Half her mouth kicked up in a smile. Obviously, she was just as excited about going out tonight as I was. "He wants to know what's taking us so long."

And just that easy, I forgot all about what we'd been talking about. Standing up, I held my hand out for her. "Come on. You sneak down first. I'll have your back. James Bond has nothing on me."

Don't miss Sebastian's story…

WHAT A BOY WANTS

Courtesy of watching his mom's relationships, Sebastian Hawkins knows what girls need to do to get a guy. He has what he considers a PhD in hooking up. When he needs extra cash for a car, Sebastian starts an online venture as The Hook-up Doctor to anonymously help girls land the guy of their dreams. Of course, his services don't offer a happily-ever-after guarantee. He's seen firsthand getting together never means staying together.

And then he falls in love . . .

With the last girl he would expect . . .

Totally not in his game plan.

Suddenly, Sebastian finds himself muddled in the game he's always prided himself on. He can't even pick up girls at parties anymore! Why would anyone want to be in love when it turns you into a stuttering, screwed-up mess with really lame stalker tendencies? Stalking? Totally not his gig.

But the Hook-up Doctor won't let himself go down easily. He's always known how to give a girl what she wants and now it's time to figure out what a boy wants . . . and he definitely plans on getting it.

headline
ETERNAL